BECOMING JAKE

by James Lee Hard

BECOMING JAKE

Edited by: Clive S. Johnson, Daisy Bank Editing Services

For questions and comments about this book, please contact the author at jamesleehard@gmail.com.

WARNING

This book contains explicit sexual scenes as well as some graphic language. It is intended for a mature, adult audience.

ISBN-13: 978-1515091363
ISBN-10: 1515091368

Acknowledgements

Thank you to my awesome beta readers for their invaluable input. Your effort and time made all the difference and the book is now much better on account of it.

So, thank you Anne Bock, Pam Kay, Tope Awofeso and Sheila Lawrence for your help on this story. **Ladies, you are awesome!**

To you, my love.

CHAPTER 1

"JAKE! COME HERE this instant!"

Jake flinched as his father's voice thundered through the PA system he had installed a couple of years before in the convenience store he owned. He had almost forgotten that cold-to-his-stomach feeling every time his dad yelled, his raspy voice full of contempt and anger. He shouldn't have returned home. A week before he had been far away, still in his college campus, dreaming of better days. Truth be told, the week before he had already been contemplating his future, thinking of how the hell he was going to make it, with no money and no career prospects. Nobody gave a shit about English majors. And yet, somehow, he had made this stupid choice of going to college to study English. He dreamed of being a writer and going to a cabin in the middle of the woods and writing all day, inspired by the lake and mountains around him—exactly like the cliché. Now he would call it an hallucination, not a dream, with his student loans looming over him, its ever presence casting a shadow on his dreams and draining his energy.

"Jake!" his father yelled again. Jake sighed, put the box he was carrying on the floor and dragged himself through the aisle. Restocking the shelves with toothpaste would have to wait.

Two days working with his father at the convenience store and he already wanted to run again and leave this town behind.

These two days had reminded him of how claustrophobic his life used to be, how suffocating his father was, how he made him feel like a useless child always getting in his way. Jake sighed deeply. Maybe he could use this anger and would rub it in the man's face that he was gay. He would tell him that not even his prayers and years of physical punishment had been successful in banning the "devil" from his body, as he used to say.

Jake had always known he was different. Not that he was intrinsically aware of it, but everyone used to point and laugh at him. He didn't understand why they did or what it was that made him so different from them. His father also used to yell at him to act like a man, not a girl. In Jake's mind he wasn't doing anything different. He simply didn't like to play football or engage in physical activities. His perfect afternoon would be spent reading a book or playing on his computer. To his father, the fact he preferred this to catching a ball was, apparently, what caused his fits.

Of course, years later Jake came to understand why his father used to yell at him to act like a man. It wasn't the books or the computer games. It was the way he moved, his gestures and his stride. He became aware of it maybe in the beginning of his teen years. He had been at a birthday party – he couldn't recall where or whose party it had been – and someone was filming it. Jake later saw the video, all the kids playing and walking around, and became intensely aware that he was different from the other boys: more delicate in his nature and in the way he expressed himself. Not effeminate, but delicate.

That had been his first clue. The others came in the form of teasing from the other kids that, later on, became harassing and bullying. When he finished high school, he was thrilled to get out of this town, to put some miles beneath his shoes and never look back. He was tired of its people's small-mindedness and not being able to be himself.

Jake left the isle. He could see his father behind the counter, gritting his teeth and pressing his lips together. Why was it that of all the places he could have gone he'd returned home, to his parent's house and the verbal abuse the man obviously missed dealing out? Yeah, he lacked the money but he could have been penniless anywhere. The country was vast and full of opportunities for young, desperate guys looking for a first, underpaid job. The only advantage of being back home was he didn't have to pay rent. That was something, right?

"Are you deaf or something? Next time don't make me call you twice."

The man was charming and Jake knew better than to answer him directly. Those weren't so much real questions as rhetorical excuses to punish him with his belt. At least, he used to when Jake was a child. Not so much anymore. He was now big enough to prevent his father from ever striking him again.

"I have to run to Mick's. My car should be ready by now. I'm also gonna check on your mother and I need you to work the counter. You think you can do that?" his father asked.

His father didn't trust him enough to work on anything other than restocking shelves but now wanted him to work the counter? That was unexpected.

"Yes, sir," he said, dragging his feet behind the counter and watching as his father left the store. A "fuck you" crossed his mind but he dismissed it immediately. He felt utterly guilty for choosing a college major that led nowhere and didn't want to pick a fight with his father and burden his mother with yet another problem. Her health wasn't in the best shape these days. The chemo was taking a toll.

Now that he thought of it, of course he didn't have any other choice but to come home. He couldn't abandon his mother now she was so sick. Besides, his home town was far enough from civilization that maybe Hunter would never find him. But he didn't want to think of Hunter or that he had basically run from him, leaving most of his things behind. Not yet, at least.

"Jake? Oh, my god. It is you!"

The high-pitched voice brought his mind back to the store. He looked up. In front of him was a woman who seemed familiar. Something about that roundish face reminded him of someone. It was obvious she knew him, judging by her giggles and wide grin. His brain clicked and he recognized the woman staring at him. It was Britta, a girl who used to be his good friend. He had fond memories of her, but as with almost everyone else from high school she didn't know he was gay and so he had just stopped emailing and texting her sometime after leaving for college. It had been his way of not dealing with the issue. In his mind, it was much easier to begin a new life somewhere else, telling people you were gay from the start, than to have to have "the talk" with your lifelong friends.

Jake didn't recall Britta being this round, though. "Britta! Look at you. It's been so long," he said, going around the counter towards her.

"I'll say. I never heard back from you."

Jake mentally winced at the remark while they hugged. "Well, you know how it is. Been really busy these past few years studying and kind of ended up neglecting old friends. Can you forgive me?" he said, smiling. He felt like a fake for pretending everything was okay with his life, that he hadn't forced himself to smile and forget about Hunter. But he wasn't faking his happiness for seeing Britta again. It was always nice to see a familiar, friendly face. Jake remembered quite well how lonely his hometown could be.

Britta dismissed his apology with a shake of her head. "Don't be silly. There's nothing to forgive. What I want to know is how are you? What have you been doing? When did you arrive? You've got to tell me everything!"

"I arrived just a couple of days ago. My mother is sick and I came back to help. Now I'm working here with my father."

"I heard about your mother," Britta said, her grin fading away. "I'm so sorry. Is she better?"

"A bit, but it's too soon to tell if the chemo is going to work."

Britta pressed her lips together. "I'm really sorry," she said, passing one finger by her watery eye.

"Thanks. Don't worry, she'll be fine." Jake paused, watching her finger. "You got married?" he asked, pointing at her finger and smiling.

Britta looked away. "A couple of years ago."

"Aww, that's nice. Didn't you plan to go to Europe and study before marriage? I think I recall you saying something about it."

"Well, sometimes life just doesn't turn out like you planned," she said while blushing and having trouble maintaining eye contact.

"I'll say…" Jake put up a half smile, trying not to seem utterly depressed about his own failed plans.

Britta shook her head like she was ridding herself of some unpleasant thought. "What are you doing tonight? We could have dinner together and catch up on all the gossip. What do you think?"

The little bell above the store door rang and someone approached the counter.

"Sure. It'll be fun," Jake said.

"Excellent! Let me give you my home address."

CHAPTER 2

THE GRANDFATHER CLOCK was ticking in the living room, its sound reverberating in the stillness of that late afternoon. From the stairs, Jake observed his father sitting on the couch. He was watching some TV show Jake couldn't recognize. Something about guns and animals and, most likely, one of those horrible shows about hunting for sport. He walked in his direction. His heart jumped and his stomach flinched. Although he wasn't a child anymore, his body still reacted in the same way it always had when he wanted to ask him something.

"Hey, dad, can I borrow the car? I'm going to meet an old friend."

"Why?"

Jake's stomach squirmed again. "I haven't seen her since I left for college and she's invited me for dinner. You remember Britta?" he asked, clenching his fists without noticing.

"What am I going to tell your mother? That you prefer to be out than here with her?"

Jake's knuckles were already white. "I don't prefer to be out. I'm just going to see an old friend."

"Words are easy, but the fact remains that you're going out."

Jake could feel his temple vein throbbing. "Can I borrow the car or not?"

"What are you boys fighting about?"

Jake turned back. His mother trudged down the stairs, white as a sheet. She seemed exhausted. He approached her, held her arm and helped her walk to the sofa. "We're not fighting, mom. I was just asking dad for the car."

His mother sat on the couch, wincing, and sighed. "Oh? Where you going?"

"Britta came by the store. Remember her? From high school? I haven't seen her in years and she invited me over for dinner."

"I remember her. She was such a lovely girl. I haven't seen her for a while, now. How is she?"

"Fine, I guess. She's married and lives nearby. We were going to catch up over dinner."

"Were? You're not going anymore?"

Jake glanced at his father. "I am. It's just a matter of driving or fetching my old bike from the garage."

His father scoffed. "Well, then, it's settled, isn't it? You do prefer to go out than stay here and help your mother."

"Steve, let the boy have some fun. He's young, he should be out and enjoying life. He doesn't need to be with me all the time."

"I think he had more than enough fun with that excuse of a degree. He should start acting like a man and think of his family."

Jake pressed his lips and chewed on the inside of his cheek, trying not to answer.

"Steve, why don't you give him the car keys and go make me some tea? I'm a bit queasy, dear."

The man got up from the couch and threw Jake the keys, mumbling something unintelligible. Jake caught them, pulling his head back instinctively and flinching his eyes. When he opened them, he saw his father sneering as he passed by.

"You have fun, sweetie. Don't you worry. I'm fine. Give my best to Britta and tell her she should visit and have some tea with us one of these days."

"I will," he said. Jake kissed his mother on the forehead and left the house. Living in his old home again was proving to be more challenging that he had expected.

***

The rain that had threatened to pour all day was now falling from the sky without compassion for anyone caught off-guard. Jake thought he might as well run for it for the shower was getting heavier by the minute. He covered his head with his coat and got out of the car, sprinting to Britta's porch. He arrived just in time. A second later the sky opened up in a heavy downpour.

Jake shook his coat and rang the doorbell, determined to come clean with Britta. He wanted to make amends and explain why he had vanished after going to college. He wanted her to know that it had nothing to do with her, that she was a lovely person. It was him who had a problem.

A man opened the door and Jake felt a warmth coming from inside the house. He ogled him instinctively, without even noticing what he was doing. The guy had copper hair, a trimmed beard, a squarish face and beautiful brown-green eyes. He reminded Jake of someone but he couldn't quite remember who. His gaze wandered over the man's torso. The tightness of his shirt revealed a very impressive physique.

The man looked at Jake with an inquisitive stare, like he was trying to remember something. "Jake?" he asked in a deep voice, smiling.

"Hi. You must be Britta's husband," Jake said, wondering why that face looked familiar. He couldn't shake the feeling that he knew the guy somehow.

"You don't remember me?" He had a wide grin on his face. "I'm Craig, from high school."

Jake's eyes widened. Craig! The beard had thrown him off but he now remembered perfectly who he was. How couldn't he? He used to have a crush on Craig back in high school and it wasn't only because of the impressive physique he'd already had back then. Craig was a really sweet guy who had always been friendly to him, unlike the guys he used to hang out with. Back then, Jake had had this feeling that Craig was always looking after him. Like one time when some jock pushed him to the ground and Craig had appeared out of nowhere, telling him it was enough. Jake remembered the guy trying to make jokes about how Craig had come to the rescue of his "girlfriend" but Craig had just stood there, staring at him, his eyes promising him the beating of his life. The bully and his buddies eventually went away, and Craig had helped Jake get up.

The Craig in front of him was like a new and improved version. Maybe he had pursued a career in football after all.

Jake's face opened in a broad smile. "I'm sorry. I didn't recognize you with that beard. Of course I remember you." His hand reached for Craig's but he received a hug instead, with a loud "come here!". Jake felt himself melting into Craig's arms and the world spun around them. His warmth penetrated Jake's skin, leaving what felt like burn marks that he didn't want to get rid of. Craig's man aroma was all around Jake, kindling a fire in his crotch like he hadn't had in a long time.

"Come in, come in," Craig said through a broad smile. "Britta's in the kitchen and asked me to come open the door. She said something about burning a cake. I'm not sure. I arrived just a minute ago."

Jake went into the house and watched Craig move ahead of him in a confident stride. He looked even better from the back, his torso wide, his bubble butt firm. Jake felt his dick twitching as a rush of lust spread throughout him.

"So, you and Britta married?" he asked casually while taking off his coat, trying not to sound too anxious about Craig's answer.

Craig's exuberant smile turned into a laugh. "No!" he answered, his brow furrowing. "Why do you think that?"

"Well, you answered the door and Britta told me she'd got married…"

"Actually, I'm visiting my dad." Craig's smile faded away. "My mom… She passed away recently and I came here to check up on him."

Jake blushed and stared at Craig, open mouthed. "Oh, I'm sorry. I didn't mean to—"

"It's okay. Don't worry. I made my peace with it."

Jake fell silent and looked down. "I can imagine what you went through," he said, thinking of his own mother.

"Let's change the subject, shall we? I don't want to bother you with this," Craig said, smiling. Jake couldn't answer him, though, as Britta had now entered the living room.

"Jake! I'm so glad you could make it. You remember Craig, right?"

Before Jake could answer, she hugged him tightly. He could smell her flowery shampoo as her head hovered slightly below his nose, and he felt her warm embrace. He had been so stupid to cut ties with her. She was a wonderful woman.

"Yeah, I remember him," Jake said, stealing a peek at Craig. His tight jeans hugged his legs and ass in such a beautiful way.

"I hope you don't mind that I've invited him for dinner. He rarely comes to visit and I couldn't pass up this opportunity."

"Of course not. It was a wonderful surprise, actually."

"Well, I have to finish supper. You kids can help yourselves to some drinks and then I expect you both in the kitchen. It can be lonely in there," Britta said, giggling. Jake watched her as she left the room and then looked around, trying to appear interested in the decor. Now he'd turned his attention to it he noticed how nice her house actually was, with a couple of bean bag chairs, a large L-shaped sofa and a modern feel to everything. Even so, the living room felt cozy. It wasn't one of those places that looked as though someone had copied a whole page out of an interior design magazine.

"So, you still live here? I don't recall Britta talking about you." Craig's voice pierced the silence that had coated the room. Jake turned around to face him.

"Not until recently. I had to move back to my parent's attic after finishing college."

"I couldn't imagine myself coming back. The mountains are beautiful, but the people here… Not so much."

"Well, you know how it is: a degree nobody cares for, student loans looming at your doorstep… I'm just loving adulthood."

Craig smiled. "I can relate to that. Even so, you are very brave to move back to your folk's. I think I recall them being very strict." He walked to a small cupboard with glass doors and started pouring himself what looked like scotch. "You want anything to drink?"

Jake nodded. "A scotch, thanks." He wasn't very fond of scotch but it seemed like an appropriate drink to have near Craig.

Am I trying to impress him or something? A little voice in his head answered *yes you are, you dumb-ass,* but he needed something strong to help him relax. He didn't know exactly why, but he felt really nervous around Craig.

"My father is not the easiest person but I'm trying to manage."

Craig gave him his drink. "Cheers," he said, raising his glass.

"Cheers," and Jake raised his own. He took a swig. The scotch burned his throat and he coughed, feeling an intense heat radiating to his face.

"Are you okay?"

"Yes," Jake managed in a hoarse voice, after a couple more coughing sessions. Through the tears, he could see Craig smiling, a slight mocking look plastered all over his face. God, but he was beautiful.

"So, I reckon drinking was on the list of things your dad didn't let you do."

"Yeah, well, Christian redneck raises his child, afraid he's going to burn in hell for having had sex with his own wife. Of course, it's only logical to blame the son for everything that's wrong in the world and keep him from sinning too much himself. Hence, no drinking."

Craig, wide-eyed, stopped midway through raising his glass to take another sip, his brow raised. Jake mentally winced, regretting what he had said. It had just slipped out. Something he had thought a million times but dared not share. Was it the scotch talking? Hardly, not after only the one taste. Anyway, he had said too much. Nobody wanted to hear about his problems.

"That came out wrong. I'm sorry. Forget it."

"Don't be." Craig stroke his beard. "I can only imagine what you've been through. My uncles were complete church freaks and made for very awkward family reunions. I think it was the way they showed you that people different from them would go straight to hell, no questions asked. They always made me feel like a sinner in their presence."

"Now imagine that every day, all day long. Except when my mother's around. She's nothing like my dad."

"I see you both have drinks," Britta said, entering the living room. "Now, could you please join me? I don't want to feel like your private chef," she said, giggling again.

Jake and Craig looked at each other and followed her back to the kitchen. For a split second, Craig's shrug and smile made Jake feel like they shared something, a teeny-tiny connection that reminded Jake of his high school days and the crush he used to have on him.

The kitchen smelled wonderful. The stove was packed with pots and pans and Jake sensed an aroma that reminded him of mustard, meat and mashed potatoes. Britta opened the oven and the previous meaty odors were replaced by the sugary scent of the cake she was baking. Jake's mouth watered and for the first time since leaving home that morning he felt hungry.

"It smells so good in here," Jake said with a big grin. There was something about that food's aroma that made him feel cozy and relaxed.

"Special food for a special occasion. I hope you boys like it," she said, closing the oven, a smile dancing in her eyes. "Could you be a darling and get me a Martini, Craig?"

"Sure."

As he left the kitchen, Britta turned to Jake. "Are you really okay with him being here? I know you tend to go along with things and say that everything is fine out of shyness. You can tell me, Jake."

Jake felt a rush of heat in his stomach. Britta had reminded him of one of the things he didn't like about himself. "It's fine, really. Don't worry. I'm actually glad you invited him over."

"Good, because I want to know everything about you. It's been years, Jake."

Jake felt the heat of a blush rush to his face.

"By the way, I really wanted to apologize to you..." Jake scratched the back of his head and switched his weight to his other leg. "I know I was a complete jerk and I shouldn't have disappeared like that—"

"It's fine. What matters is that you're here now."

"No, it's not fine. I wanted to..." Jake scratched the back of his head again. "I wanted you to know that it wasn't because of you. You were a really good friend to me in high school but... I had...I was going through some stuff I was too embarrassed to share with—"

"If this is about you being gay, you should know I totally support you, Jake. It doesn't change a thing about how I feel about you."

Jake's mouth had dropped opened. "You knew?"

"Jake, it doesn't take a rocket scientist, you know? You were shy and sensitive and I've never seen you interested in a girl. Of course I knew. I have to say that, back then, I felt a bit hurt you didn't tell me, but I get that you just needed some time. Water under the bridge, as far as I'm concerned."

A rustling sound made Jake turn his head. Craig was by the kitchen door, a Martini in his hand.

"Sorry. I didn't mean to intrude..."

Jake's ears felt very hot. He wanted to flee but then remembered he wasn't in high school anymore and there was no need to hide from his friends. "You're not intruding." He took a sip of whiskey in the hopes the drink would help ease his intense discomfort. Instead, he felt his throat burning.

"I know it's uncomfortable to come out to your friends. I personally feel it's easier to do it to strangers, actually," Craig said.

Jake almost choked on his scotch.

"Oh, my gosh! Enough with this dance, already," Britta said. "Jake, you're both gay. Can we move on to things that *really* matter? I'm starving!"

Jake's heart raced at the revelation. Maybe this explained why Craig used to be so nice to him in high school. Maybe it had been his way of telling him he wasn't alone, that he was gay too.

"Now I feel even more embarrassed for not telling you everything back in high school," he said, looking down.

"Don't be," Britta said, approaching Jake and hugging him. "I know how this town is, honey. It's all water under the bridge, okay?"

Jake smiled and nodded, feeling relieved. Britta smiled back and turned to the stove, stirring the mashed potatoes.

Once again the situation had proven to him that most of the time people didn't care if he was gay or not. It only mattered how decent a person he was.

His phone buzzed and Jake's stomach did a somersault. Nobody had his number but Matt, one of his few friends in college. He had changed numbers because of Hunter and now felt like the world would come to an end every time his phone chimed.

He looked at its screen, his hands shaking.

Hi. Just wanted to warn you that Hunter might know where you are. I was taking a shower and my flatmate let him in. When I got to my bedroom, he was in there and I could swear my phone wasn't in the same place. I hope I'm just being paranoid.

The ice Jake had felt when the phone buzzed now settled fully in his chest, gut and legs. He knew that sooner or later Hunter would find out where he was, but had hoped that somehow he'd have had enough money by then to get out of here and disappear to somewhere far away. Now it was just a matter of time until Hunter appeared on his doorstep.

"Is everything okay? You look pale." Britta was looking at him with worry written across her face.

Jake's first reaction was to tell her about Hunter but he decided against it. He felt embarrassed and didn't want to spoil the night.

"I'm fine. Just a bit tired."

"What you need is to put some food in that belly!"

"Should we wait for your husband?"

"Yeah, where is Eric?"

Britta opened her mouth but for a second said nothing. She seemed hesitant but then her usual smile came back. "He called and apologized, but he's stuck at work. So, more food for us."

CHAPTER 3

THE NIGHT ENDED up being far more enjoyable than Jake had anticipated, and although he had to leave early, he felt happy. Not even the fact that Hunter was probably on his way there or that he had to get up at six in the morning to open the store and work beside his father could upset him right now.

He parked the car in the driveway and went inside his parents' house. The kitchen lights were on and he prayed it was not his father. He wasn't in the mood to talk with him.

"Mom? What are you doing up? You should be resting."

"Oh, hi, honey. You scared me. I didn't hear you arrive," his mother said, grabbing her chest with one hand. "I felt like having some tea. My stomach's still a little upset."

Jake placed the food Britta had given him on the counter. "Here, let me do that for you." He grabbed the kettle while his mother sat on the counter stool next to where she'd been standing. She was still pale and he noticed she had some trouble breathing, like she was exhausted just by sitting there. "Why didn't you ask dad to prepare you the tea?"

"You know how your father is. He can't tell a kettle from a pot."

Jake frowned. "That's because you did everything around here."

"Jake…"

"It's true. Has he even learned how to cook anything so you can rest? At least while you're on the chemo?"

"Jake, please. You know I don't like it when you talk like that. Don't disrespect your father."

Jake put the kettle on the stove and turned it on. "I'm not being disrespectful, mom, I'm just telling the truth."

His mother didn't answer back. "How was dinner at Britta's? Did you have fun?"

As usual, she had changed the subject. It was one of her many skills as the house's diplomat, learned after years of living with a man who wouldn't listen to anyone's opinion. Jake could see she was unwell and decided not to pursue the subject. He took a deep breath before answering. "It was great, actually. Really good to see old friends. Oh, she cooked too much food and sent some for you. I told her you weren't well enough to cook," he said, putting a tea bag in a mug.

"How nice of her. Give her my regards the next time you see her."

"What's all this racket about? Don't you know your mother has to rest?"

His father had just entered the kitchen, yelling. Jake felt a rush of heat to his ears and his heart pumping hard. He ground his teeth before answering: "I'm just making mom some tea."

"Next time keep it down. You woke me up and I have a store to open up in the morning."

"I'm sorry that mother's cancer is disturbing your sleep…"

His father was already leaving but stopped in his tracks. He turned around and approached Jake, stopping inches from his face, a menacing glare in his eyes. "What did you say?"

For a split second, the thought of punching this horrible, selfish man in the face crossed Jake's mind. Behind them, his mother watched, as pale as ever, big dark patches below her eyes, worry creases forming across her forehead.

"Nothing."

"I thought so," he said proudly, as if he'd won yet another battle and proved who was the alpha male in his own house. "I'm warning you, boy: unless you want to sleep out on the street, you'd better watch your tongue. Now let your mother rest."

Jake watched him as he left, and shuddered with rage. He immediately thought of leaving the house. No debt justified going through that kind of abuse. He had no right treating him like a brat who didn't know his place. His gaze travelled to his mother. She looked frailer than ever. His frustration evaporated and his shoulders relaxed. She needed his help. He couldn't just abandon her.

"I'm sorry. I didn't mean to upset you, mom," Jake said, after a deep breath.

"You know you can't talk to your father like that, Jake. You owe him more respect."

"I owe him nothing! I'm here for you, mom, not because of him."

"Jake, don't be like this. You know the good Lord said to honor your father—"

"Mom, please. I don't want to fight with you. I'm sorry, but I can't respect someone who is so Christian and loving of God to the neighbors but can't do what he preaches inside his own house. If I'm breaking the Lord's commandments, it's because he broke them first. Wasn't he supposed to love his son? What have I ever done to him?"

His mother faced him in silence. The kettle whistled and Jake thanked it for that. He could see the disappointment in his mother's eyes and was too afraid it was due to him being gay.

He grabbed the kettle and poured the hot water in the cup, giving his mother her tea.

"I'm going upstairs. Long day tomorrow." He kissed her on the forehead and left the kitchen.

He walked up the narrow stairs to the attic in long strides, clenching his fists. He didn't know how much more of his father's abuse he could bear. The night had been so enjoyable up until that moment. The good food, the fact he'd felt welcomed by Britta and Craig and a general sense of belonging made him regret even more his decision to cut his ties with his friends. It had just been stupid.

Craig came into his mind again, warming his insides and making him forget his father for a second. He wished he'd known about Craig being gay back in high school. Maybe he would have acted on his crush and told him about his feelings, and how Craig made him hard at night, under the blankets.

As soon as this thought crossed his mind, he scoffed at it. It was totally ridiculous to think he would have done anything, even if he had known about Craig. Hell, he could barely talk to him *now* without blushing and choking on his own words. Back then he was a very quiet kid who had always tried to blend in with the walls and shadows, always fleeing from unnecessary social interactions.

Jake entered the attic. The light from the streetlamp outside seeped through the window, casting shadows all over the room. He didn't know why but this felt pleasant to him. He tossed his coat on a chair. Maybe he could do something about his crush now, but would he have the guts to? He looked out the window. It had started raining again. He shook his head. Jake knew he wouldn't have the nerve to do it but it was good to fantasize about anyway. Especially given Craig was so damn hot; even hotter than back in high school.

He went into the bathroom while trying to cast Craig's image from his mind. He looked into the mirror and thanked his genes for being a half-decent guy, body-wise. He had been in and out of the gym in the past few years but knew it had nothing to do with his fairly lean frame. Most of the time he didn't even break a sweat. Even so, guys used to tell him he had a nice ass and body, although he didn't quite believe them. Receiving a compliment wasn't something that came naturally to Jake or was easy to accept. Another quirk he could thank his father for, after years of continued "You can't do anything right, can you?".

Would Craig find him interesting enough should he decide to act on his crush? Jake shook his head and started brushing his teeth. What was he thinking? He had so much in his life right now. He couldn't afford to be distracted by his own dick. He had to think of what to do if Hunter really was on his way. He shuddered at the thought but, somehow, Craig's solid physique sneaked into his mind again and he felt a shiver run down his spine. Craig's shirt suggested he was all muscle beneath the fabric, a proper strong man able to grab you and make the whole world go away. It wasn't that hard to let his imagination go wild given that Craig had rolled up his sleeves during dinner and Jake had seen how toned he was. Maybe not as much as the guys he looked up online; maybe his pecs and abs weren't as defined, but he didn't care for those guys, anyway. And even if Craig wasn't a cover model, he was most definitely a man capable of igniting Jake's desire. There was something in the way his gaze had perused him while they talked, his manly figure, his confident attitude... Craig was all man wrapped in a package of kindness, sporting a beautiful smile. Who could resist that?

Jake felt a knot in his throat as he dried his hands and mouth with the towel. Craig's tight jeans had teased him all night with a promise of delicious treats underneath. That bulge, the way the fabric hugged him and seemed almost too weak to resist whatever lurked beneath, the idea of what could be there sent an electric jolt down to his crotch. An intense heat radiated from there as his own dick pressed against his jeans.

He grabbed his cock and squeezed it through the fabric. It jumped again and an intense desire overran him. He went to the bedroom and took his sweatshirt and shoes off as fast as he could, tossing the clothes into a corner. His dick throbbed in anticipation as he grabbed it. He lay on the bed and stroked it with strong, rapid hand movements, feeling the urgency of his arousal grow with each one. The world around him disappeared. His dick was hungry for Craig, for a release Jake hadn't desired for so long. Before he knew it, his mind retreated inside himself. He could only feel the geyser deep down within him expanding with each stroke, impossible to stop. He came all over himself, gusts of warm cum shooting over his belly.

Jake panted, trying to catch his breath, fleeting thoughts of how he hadn't felt an orgasm this intense for so long running through his mind. He was relaxed and drowsy, and felt himself drift into sleep, his hand still grabbing a now deflating cock, trying to extend the rush of pleasure he had just felt. An image of Hunter arriving in town appeared out of nowhere but he didn't care. Not even Hunter would rob him of a few more moments of total bliss.

CHAPTER 4

HE COULDN'T QUITE see the man in front of him. The shape of his face was out of focus but he could still see his smile. It was a warm smile, one that made him feel all cozy inside. The guy was handsome, although he didn't know how he knew this. His strong arms were waving at him, telling him to move closer, inviting his fingers to explore every detail of his sinewy body. Jake moved in and a heat wave spread through him as he touched the man's chest, his own bulging dick pressing hard against his pants, wanting to be freed. He grabbed the man by his ass and moved in closer, pinning him against the wall with his crotch. He panted as a rush of arousal took over and concentrated on his throbbing dick.

He leaned in, his lips brushing against the man's, when a strong, high-pitched sound pierced the air. He tried to ignore it, to focus on the man's musky aroma and warm lips, but the sound kept growing inside his head. He couldn't stand it anymore. He just wanted it to go away.

***

Jake almost jumped out of bed. His heart drummed in his ears and a surge of adrenaline ran through his veins, making his stomach cold.

What the hell was that noise?

He now barely registered the dream he'd just had about Craig. The frail image was already losing its strength as he looked around, trying to figure out where the sound was coming from. The dream state his mind was in slowly faded away and he realized he was in his bedroom and the alarm clock had sounded off.

"Piece of crap," he muttered to himself. He reached his arm out to turn the damn thing off and took a deep breath while rubbing his forehead. He was trying to remember the reason his alarm clock was going off at six o'clock in the morning, but his brain was foggy and slow, and he couldn't.

Oh, yeah. The store. He groaned and rubbed his eyes. The last thing he wanted was to be in the same place with his father all day, under his controlling and judgmental stare.

Jake tugged the comforter away in one sharp movement and got up, putting on his T-shirt and boxer shorts. He approached the window and opened the curtains. The mountain range along the horizon was getting brighter but the night still hadn't gone away. The sky was filled with dark, thick clouds, promising another day heavy with rain. He scratched his butt and took a deep breath while looking outside. A shiver ran through him. The hair on his thighs stood on end with the cold. He rubbed his legs to generate some heat and his stomach flinched with a cramp. He held his breath, waiting for it to pass, but it didn't. Instead, the cramp strengthened and his stomach hurt.

What the hell? Just what I needed.

Jake went back to the bed, walking a little bent to ease the pain. He covered himself with the duvet and put his knees to his chest, holding on to them with his arms. Maybe if he stayed in this foetal position the pain would go away.

His stomach throbbed and Jake winced. Lately, his gut had been acting funky. He didn't know why but suspected it had something to do with stress. But why was it acting out now?

Oh, right. Hunter.

The memory from the previous night flooded him. His brain was now fully awake. Jake felt his stomach squeezing and burning like he had a couple of embers inside him. He still didn't know what he'd do if Hunter really was on his way.

This has got to be your worst mistake to date, you ass, he thought to himself as his stomach continued to burn.

"Jake! Are you awake? Hurry up in there. The store isn't going to open up by itself. We have to go," a strong, raspy voice said.

Jake grimaced as his stomach again twitched in pain. "I can't go," he said, as loud as he could.

His father opened the door. "What?"

"I can't go today. My stomach hurts."

"Your stomach hurts? What kind of excuse is that?"

Jake's stomach twisted and a sharp pain pierced the left side of his gut. "It's not an excuse," he insisted, taking slow, deep breaths as he spoke. "I don't know what happened."

His father approached the bed. "Isn't this great? Two days of real work and you're already sick. Your mother really spoiled you." He shook his head, turned around and walked to the door. "It serves you right for leaving her last night," he said before leaving the room and slamming the door behind him.

***

Jake spent most of the morning lying in bed. He'd dragged himself to the kitchen after his father had left and made himself a cup of tea in the hopes the hot liquid would help with his cramps. It eventually did, so he decided the best thing to do would be to go to the store. He wanted to avoid more drama in the event his father realized he'd gotten better around noon.

"You sure you feel better?" his mother asked as he kissed her on the forehead.

"Yes, I feel fine now. I'll see you in a bit."

He left the house, lost in his own thoughts as he walked to the store. It was one of the few things he'd actually missed about this place. He could walk everywhere if he really wanted to. Of course, this was also a problem. In a small town like this, Hunter would have no trouble finding his parents' house. Maybe he should talk to them before he arrived. Jake didn't know what he'd do but suspected the worst. And the worst would be being outed by him, especially now his mother was sick. That wouldn't help her recovery.

Someone bumped into him and Jake was flung out of his thoughts. He looked up. In front of him were two guys who seemed to be about the same age as himself, both smirking at him.

"Well, look who it is," one of them said.

"Jake B.J., the fag from high school," the other added.

Jake's stomach somersaulted and for a moment he felt his cramps returning. He recognized their faces instantly. Tom and Kevin, two of the high school assholes that loved to pick on him. They were like a scar in his memory, although he'd worked hard to forget about them after years of their bullying.

"Hello to you too," he said, fuming and clenching his fists. He recalled how he had tried to avoid them back in high school, but was always somehow bumping into them on the streets. One of the problems of small towns like this.

"What you doing here?" Tom said. "I thought you'd left to be gay in some fancy big city."

"Maybe he came to visit his boyfriend. What was his name?" Kevin slapped Tom's shoulder. "Craig! You remember? The jock?"

"Oh, yeah. The prince charming that was always saving his damsel in distress. Does he live here?" Tom asked, looking at Kevin and scratching his head like the idiot he was.

"Can you get out of my way?" Jake tried to side-step them, but the two guys blocked his way like they used to and, for a brief moment, Jake was fourteen again.

"Aww, you have to go? What if I paid you to stay, huh? Would you blow me?" Tom said, grabbing his crotch and jiggling his bulge in Jake's direction. Kevin laughed, with short, high-pitched guffaws.

Jake felt disgusted by them both. They were the epitome of rednecks, with their squinty, little blue eyes, squared, freckled faces and piggy noses. Several images of him punching them in the face ran through his mind, but he wasn't strong enough for that. He didn't remember ever having punched anyone and he certainly wouldn't start now.

"You want me to suck your dick? For you I'll do it for free. Just whip it out. Come on, right here. Doesn't it turn you on?" he said, advancing on Tom, speaking in loud whispers, his mouth barely open, like he was turned on by him. In reality, he was furious and that had been the only thing that had occurred to him to do. Now he'd done it, though, he realized it had been a very stupid idea.

"What the fuck, dude?" Tom screeched, jumping back. "Get away from me!"

"Fuckin' homo," Kevin added, the corner of his lips pulled up in disgust.

Jake's cheeks were a shade of deep red and his breathing was fast. He wanted to hurt them and make them beg for mercy. Instead, he walked on by, never losing the two idiots from sight, a heavy frown ornamenting his face. It always had been his way of trying to intimidate bullies and he still did it.

"Can you believe this guy?" Tom asked, slapping Kevin on his shoulder with the back of his hand, as Jake walked away. "Go suck on your boyfriend, fag."

"Yeah, and keep your homo lifestyle away from us. I bet that's why your mother's got cancer. She prefers to die than to have a son like you." Kevin snickered and looked at Tom like he had made the best joke ever.

Something snapped inside Jake and he stopped in his tracks. Before realizing it, he'd thrown himself onto Kevin, pulled his arm back and punched him with a strength driven by anger. Kevin was still snickering when Jake hit him, catching him off-guard, losing his balance and taking a couple of steps back, trying not to fall. But Jake kept going, and before Kevin could react, he was already punching him again. And again. His insides boiled and the world in front of him became hard to grasp. He couldn't think. He could only hear the injustice of what these two idiots kept babbling.

"Don't ever talk about my mother's cancer again, you piece of shit!" he bellowed, maddened by their ignorance and fuelled by a rage stored up over the many years they had picked on him.

Tom grabbed Jake's arms from behind, pulled him away from Kevin and pushed him back. Jake almost fell but managed to keep his balance. He was already advancing again, this time on Tom, but who now pulled a knife from his jacket.

"What're you kids doing?" an old woman shouted from across the street.

Tom turned to her as he hid his knife again. "See you next time, faggot," he said out of the corner of his mouth in a menacing tone. "Come on." Tom grabbed Kevin by his arm and they hurried along the street.

Jake was left there, panting. A moment later, a sharp pain radiated from his right hand. It was slightly bruised. He grabbed it, trying to ease the pain. Punches hurt a lot more than they made you believe in movies.

CHAPTER 5

JAKE ARRIVED AT the store slightly disheveled. He was still fuming over those rednecks. What kind of people would say hurtful things like that? He took a deep breath and tried to calm himself down. This was still one of his weaknesses: injustice, or what he perceived as injustice, would send him on a rampage of ill-advised behavior. This wasn't just perceived, though. This was beyond stupidity and utterly maddening.

"Ah, I see you're up to doing some work. Good. I have some boxes for you to unpack," his father said, looking up from the sheet of paper he had on top of the counter. He didn't comment on his untidy appearance and Jake didn't say a thing either. He went into the backroom in silence, ruminating over what had happened.

He closed the door and let the silence invade him. He noticed his hands were shaking and drew them closer to his eyes. The one he'd used to punch Kevin still hurt but the bruise hadn't spread and was now hardly visible. He put his hands down and paced the room, taking big, deep breaths, trying to relax. The shaking of his hands spread, though, and a minute later he was shuddering and felt cold. A couple of tears rolled down his face without him noticing and the world grew into something sterile and threatening. He wiped the tears away with the back of his hand and closed his eyes. He had to fight that feeling. Every time something like this happened,

Jake was invaded by dread, this cold, low-hum feeling of threat that latched itself to his skin, penetrated him and buried itself deep, freezing his guts and legs. He had to fight it or else everything wrong in his life would be amplified and transformed into a life-threatening menace. He took another deep breath, trying to ignore the whirlpool of negative thoughts that always feasted on him at times like this.

Hunter appeared in his mind and Jake stopped pacing and coughed when a bit of spit inadvertently slid to his windpipe. He had to calm himself. He shouldn't be stressing over something hypothetical. Maybe Hunter would just give up and let him go, even if he had seen where he was living. He started pacing again. Who was he kidding? Hunter wouldn't let go, he knew that. He was too obsessed with Jake to forget. *What am I going to do?* He couldn't just leave his mother. That was completely out of the question. On the other hand, he didn't want to think of what could happen if Hunter did arrive in town.

Jake felt trapped in a maze of problems, no solution in sight. The room spun and he thought the crates and boxes would fall onto him. Closing his eyes, he held on to one of the metal shelves and let its cold seep in, steadying his breathing. He could hear his heartbeat drumming in his ears and his stomach clenching and threatening to hurt like hell. In the vortex that were his thoughts, he saw Craig and his solid frame. He recalled his manly aroma, that heavenly scent that invaded him and lit a fire within him. And his smile; his warm, welcoming smile that was everything. He opened his eyes, feeling a bit more relaxed.

You can do this. He grabbed the boxes his father had asked for and left the storage room.

"Oh, there you are. I was starting to wonder if you had gone in there to take a nap."

The relaxation Jake had managed to muster evaporated instantly. "Will you please give me a break? Do you have to be constantly bickering with me? Did you even notice that I arrived here looking like I'd been mugged?" Jake said, almost shouting. The few customers in the store looked up from the products they were examining and Jake felt their gaze on his nape. His father was mute and pale, staring at him, wide-eyed. His paleness lasted only a brief moment, though, and was quickly replaced by a crimson red.

"You better show me some respect, you hear me? Don't you ever dare speak to me in that tone again," his father said, an angry finger pointing towards Jake.

Jake's blood was making a marching band noise in his eardrums, his heart thumping in his chest. He wanted to smack him in the head, make him see how awful he was, but at the same time he felt deeply saddened by the fact that this was the only relationship he could have with his father.

He bit his tongue and thought of his mother. He had to control himself and learn to let go. "I'm sorry, sir. It won't happen again."

"You damn right it won't." The man studied him attentively. "What happened anyway? You look like a hobo."

"I slipped and fell on the sidewalk."

"Well, go restock the shelves. And tidy yourself up. I don't want you scaring the customers away."

Jake gritted his teeth and sighed deeply before turning away and leaving. He tried to relax again, concentrating on the noise of his breathing, but it didn't work. So he tried to recall the image of Craig again. *Why have I been constantly thinking of him since yesterday?* He put the box on the floor. *A guy like him must have a ton of hot guys chasing him. So, there. Just stop it before it's too late and your old feelings for him come rushing back in.* Old habits die hard? Whatever, at least he'd realized what he was doing and was happy he'd caught it in time. It was better to stop it now than to suffer later, wondering why decent guys were completely out of his league.

CHAPTER 6

JAKE SPENT THE rest of his day trying hard not to think of Craig. As much as he fought it, though, the image of him would pop up in his mind when he least expected it. Things didn't improve the next day. He was restocking a shelf absent-mindedly, his mind wondering between Craig and the certainty that working at his father's store hadn't been his brightest idea. It had been naïve of him to think that helping here would be an opportunity to make amends and show his father he was willing to make things right. It just wasn't working out. It didn't matter if Jake was willing to forgive his father because he sure as hell didn't seem prepared to accept this white flag of truce. Maybe it would be best just to leave the house and the store and look for a job elsewhere. He could continue visiting and helping his mother. Maybe this way things with his father would cool off enough to prevent him from saying something he'd later regret. This meant he'd have to start paying rent, though, and right now every dime he made was going to repay his debt.

"So, this is where you work."

Jake almost jumped out of his skin. His mind had been so far away he hadn't heard the customer arrive. He turned to find Craig standing before him, his warm smile inviting Jake to lose himself in it and let go of everything.

"Hey. Didn't hear you arrive."

"Sorry to sneak up on you. I didn't mean to."

"No, that's all right. My mind was just somewhere else."

"Is it something I can help you with?"

The first thought that crossed Jake's mind was that Craig could start by taking his shirt off and then hugging him tight. "It's fine, thanks. What are you doing here?"

"I need toothpaste. I forgot to bring mine and my father has the worst taste in these things." Craig's grin was contagious. Jake just wanted to smile back and forget about his problems.

"It's just over there, to the left," Jake said, pointing to the end of the aisle.

"Thanks." Craig paused for a moment, like he was going to say something, but then just smiled. This time, though, it wasn't warm, more like someone trying to disguise his embarrassment. Jake recognized it immediately. After all, he was the master of embarrassed smiles.

A second later, Craig still hadn't said anything, the awkwardness palpable. Jake could feel it oozing around them, thickening the air and making it hard to breathe. He felt compelled to speak, to say something.

"Britta's an excellent cook, isn't she?" He'd said the first thing he could think of but regretted it immediately. It was just dumb and almost as bad as commenting on the weather.

"Oh, my goodness. So good. And those mashed potatoes. Yum." Craig put his hands in his jean's pockets.

"Yeah... I liked the cake. The cake was good."

"It was..."

Jake was out of ideas. He didn't know what was going on or what to say. For a second, he thought this would be the moment to act on his crush, like he had fantasized two nights before, but he couldn't. It was ridiculous even to think of it.

Besides, he had decided not to pursue those thoughts because he didn't want to suffer later on.

"So, I have to get back to work or my father's gonna kill me – literally. And I normally don't use the word 'literally' to express a strong feeling about anything, even when it's not true—" In his head, Jake was thinking he should just stop talking. "—I just hate when people talk like dumb teenagers… It's just I'm afraid of him doing it for real…"

"I can imagine…"

"Anyway, I should get back to this."

"Sure. Well, it was nice to see you again."

"You too."

Craig walked past Jake towards the end of the aisle, but stopped and turned back. "Listen, would you like to have a drink with me one of these days?" he asked in one go, exhaling as he spoke.

Jake was caught off-guard and felt himself flush at the unexpected invitation. He looked at Craig, open mouthed, like he had forgotten how to speak. "Sure… I mean, yes I'd like that," he ended up saying, remembering to draw the corner of his lips up, despite his shock.

"Great. I'll call you." Craig turned around and walked down the aisle. He seemed happy.

Jake watched him go off to find the toothpaste, nailed to the ground and speechless. His heart raced and his mind filled with thoughts of the two of them together, walking down the street, holding hands, sharing ideas, kissing… He was being childish, of course, but he couldn't help himself. He'd never had a guy like Craig hitting on him before. Was it, though? Was Craig hitting on him or just being friendly? It was perfectly reasonable to think he just wanted to hang out.

Once again, you're thinking too much and will end up winding yourself up in wishful thinking. Jake shook his head while lecturing himself, thinking he couldn't get a guy like Craig in a million years. *But why not? Are you implying he's shallow? Why couldn't you get a guy like him? Just because he's hunky and you're not?* Jake shook his head again. *Oh, my God. I'm doing it again, talking to myself. I should be committed.*

"Jake! Can you come here for a minute?" His father's voice thundered through the PA system. Jake shuddered when he heard his name. His father seemed angry.

What now?

Jake hurried along the aisle, wondering why the man was so upset. He recalled everything he had done so far, every shelf he'd restocked, every sheet he'd filled in, and couldn't think of anything he might have done wrong. But it was impossible to foresee problems with his father, as his mind worked on different logic.

He was a couple of steps from the counter when he saw a man standing beside his father, his head moving around, checking out the store. Jake's nose was hit by a revolting perfume and his gut clenched. He recognized the man immediately. The world spun around Jake and he felt sick to his stomach. His legs faltered, refusing to carry him further, and so he steadied himself on a shelf. He stood there for what seemed like an eternity, incapable of moving. His brain was having problems accepting what he was seeing and his body wasn't willing to help in any way.

Hunter.

Ever since he'd received that text from Matt he'd been expecting this moment, but up until now his mind had created the illusion of it being a distant possibility, some hypothetical scenario where his world would come to a screeching halt and he'd be forced to confront the very man he was running from. But this wasn't some possibility that could or couldn't happen.

This was real. This was Hunter in his father's store, looking around with his typical smugness. His father was observing him, frowning and tapping his fingers hard on the counter, sighing heavily. Jake dreaded what Hunter could've told him. He didn't want to know. He just wanted to leave, to get out of there and never look back.

His father looked straight at Jake, piercing him, glinting with a malice he hadn't seen before. There were no other customers around, and for a second Jake's old habit of being afraid of approaching him kicked in.

"Can you explain the meaning of this?" he barked, his finger pointing at Jake's former boyfriend. Hunter heard him speaking and turned around. A big, expansive smile appeared on his face, doubling the amount of smugness he usually wore.

Such an asshole.

"I'm not following you, sir" Jake said, trying to buy some time. It was hopeless, though. He was certain that whatever Hunter had told him was beyond repair.

"What do you mean, 'I'm not following you'? Are you making fun of me? Why is this man telling me he's your boyfriend? What's the meaning of this? I didn't raise you to be a faggot!"

That level of profanity was through the roof, which meant there was no turning back. Soon enough his father would start yelling some verse from the Bible and threatening him with the fires of hell.

"I'm sorry, Jake. I assumed your family knew about you," Hunter said, a false tone of regret in his voice.

Assumed my ass. He knew perfectly well his father was a Christian redneck and that Jake wasn't out to his family yet.

Jake's gaze hopped from his father to Hunter and back again. He was at a loss for words. He wanted to yell that they could both go fuck themselves but somehow he stayed mute.

Neither his tongue nor his brain would cooperate in producing any meaningful sound.

"Well?" his father barked again.

"He's not my boyfriend," Jake finally managed to say.

"Of course I'm your boyfriend, Jake. I was worried sick about you—"

"Stop, Hunter. Just stop. You shouldn't have come here."

"Well, you gave me no choice when you ran away like that, now did you?" Hunter said in a half-smile while scratching his neck.

"No choice? What does that even mean?" Jake asked, furrowing his brow and shrugging his shoulders. "Can't you learn how to respect what I want, Hunter? Just leave!"

"I'm not leaving without you. You need to come home, baby."

Jake saw his father go to the counter to fetch the gun he hid in there. He returned, cocking it and pointing it at Hunter's head. Jake had never seen that expression on his father's face, a mixture of anger and repulsion. The frozen glare in his eyes also told Jake he'd shoot without giving it a second thought should Hunter not do as he'd been told.

"Get the hell out of my store, you sodomite!"

Hunter jumped back a step and held his hands in front of him. "Calm down, mister. Don't do anything you'll later regret."

"The only thing I'll regret is having you around. Now, get the fuck out!" He made a menacing gesture towards Hunter who hurriedly backed away. He took one final look at Jake and left the convenience store.

Jake's heartbeat was muffling the noises around him. He'd registered his father yelling at Hunter with a gun pointed at his head, but it all came in from a distance, like he was submerged in water. He saw his father go after Hunter and slam the store's door and then return, shouting at him while he put the gun back behind the counter.

"You can start by explaining yourself!"

Jake's brain had turned on the sounds around him once more. He was about to speak when a movement caught his eye. Craig was approaching them from one of the farthest aisles, walking with hesitant steps. He seemed both scared and embarrassed as he approached the counter, a tube of toothpaste in his hand.

"I'll leave this here and return another time," he stuttered as he placed the toothpaste on the counter. Before leaving the store he glanced at Jake. His eyes seemed sad but Jake couldn't tell for sure. A moment later and Craig was gone.

CHAPTER 7

JAKE HAD WATCHED Craig leave the store. For a second, he'd worried Craig might think he had a boyfriend but these thoughts were quickly dislodged by his father's rage. A slap to his jaw knocked him out of his stupor. His head banged on a shelf and Jake felt dizzy as the whole store spun around him.

"I didn't raise you to be a sodomite! Do you have any idea what this will do to your mother? What kind of perverted sickness has taken hold of you? I knew I shouldn't have let you go to that college on the east coast. Land of perverted sinners!"

Jake opened and closed his mouth a couple of times, to see if it was still in the right place, while feeling it with his hand. A ringing sound in his right ear muffled the world but he could still hear his father shouting at him. His upper lip was curved in disgust while he talked about sinners and sodomites, and how Jake had shamed his family.

Jake tried to recall a time when he hadn't been afraid of his father's fury, of what the man could do to him. He couldn't. His father was more like one of the bullies from high school than a loving and caring parent.

Jake felt detached from the moment. He realized their relationship was now fundamentally broken. His father had never respected or treated him in a loving way, and yet he'd always tried to do as he was told, hoping that somehow he could elicit more than anger from the man.

Enough was enough.

"Don't you ever dare touch me again," Jake yelled.

His father froze, open-mouthed, watching him with what could only be a shocked expression. "You little—" He approached Jake, his hand flying out to strike him again, but Jake stopped him with ease and shoved him away, realizing his father wasn't the strong man he used to be; that Jake could defend himself and not get beaten up.

"I said don't touch me again. I'm not a small child anymore. I'm a man and I demand you treat me with some respect!"

His father's face was flushed, his jaw clenched. Jake noticed a vein throbbing in his neck as he panted, looking at him like he was judging the situation, trying to see if he could still have the upper hand.

"Man?" He laughed maniacally while dragging his feet to the counter. "You're no man and you never were. I could tell from the beginning you had the devil in you, with your effeminate ways and your delicate nature. I sure as hell tried to beat it out of you, but apparently I couldn't."

Jake's breathing was now fast and shallow. He felt as if his father had been successful in punching him again. He couldn't believe what he was hearing.

"How can you be such a horrible person? Doesn't that Bible of yours teach you to be nice or something?"

"You're an abomination and God doesn't like abominations!"

There it was, plastered in front of him in all its grotesque glory, so he could see the truth. And the truth was his father hated him.

Jake felt a knot in his throat and his eyes welled up with tears. He didn't want to cry, he didn't want this man having the final satisfaction of being able to point out to him that he was so weak that crying was the only thing he knew how to do. Jake fought it with all his strength but could feel the tears threatening to overflow and wash him with sorrow. It was so sad and hurtful to have someone spit that kind of bile at you, to say to your face how much they hated you, especially when it came from someone close to you. What had he done to deserve it?

His father shook his head and scoffed. "You can't even listen to the truth without crying. I'm embarrassed to say you're my son. Your lifestyle, your choices have brought me nothing but disgust."

Jake wiped a couple of tears from his eyes with the back of his hand. "Lifestyle? Don't you get it? It's not a lifestyle. I didn't choose this. Do you really think I like being humiliated? That I enjoy having my own father calling me an abomination? Have you stopped to think of that? Or is your head so far up your ass in embarrassment, worried what the neighbors would say?" Jake let a sob escape when he saw his father's sigh, his face revealing his true reasons. "So that's why you hate me so much. You're afraid of what the neighbors might think of *you*!"

"I should not have let you return home. Your mother deserves better."

It was Jake's turn to scoff. "Oh, you're absolutely right. Mom deserves way better. Unfortunately, she only has you! You know what...?" He strode to the coat hanger behind the counter and picked up his jacket.

"Where do you think you're going? You still have work to do," his father shouted.

"Do it yourself. I'm leaving."

"Come here. You hear me?"

Jake answered him by banging the door behind him.

***

Jake looked at the house where he had grown up and felt broken inside. It was one thing to think about leaving your old life and never looking back, but actually to do it felt definitive, like reality had suddenly fallen on his head with a weight of a thousand trucks.

He knew his mother would be inside but he didn't want to see her. It would be too hard to talk with her now. He entered the house, trying not to make any noise, and sneaked upstairs to the attic. She was probably still recovering from her last chemo treatment.

Jake entered his bedroom and looked around. His life was once again upside down, a jumbled mess like the pile of clothes in the corner. He thought that running away from Hunter would make his life less horrible, but it had achieved nothing. He could run all he wanted to but his problems would always follow suit.

He looked for his duffel bag and threw some clothes in. He couldn't carry everything with him and didn't know if his father would let him pick up the rest afterwards, but it didn't matter. He just wanted to leave and avoid a confrontation with him inside the house. His mother was too sick to watch his father calling him an abomination.

Jake zipped the bag and approached the door, taking one last look around his room. Beyond the window he could see the day was as cloudy as his mood. It might rain. Where would he go?

With a final sigh, he left the attic, wondering what to do next.

"Jake? What are you doing here, honey?"

His mother was leaving her bedroom as he stepped off the attic stairs. She was pale and seemed frail, as usual. Jake looked at her without knowing what to say.

"What's that bag for? Are you going somewhere?" The small wrinkles at the side of her eyes were now more pronounced. She was clearly worried.

"I'm leaving."

She tilted her head. "What are you saying, Jake? You're leaving?" She was getting paler as she spoke.

"Something happened at the store… I can't stay here anymore. I'm sorry. I love you, mom."

"What happened at the store? Tell me!"

He was already going down the stairs to the living room, but stopped. He looked at his mother's imploring eyes and knew he couldn't leave without an explanation. Despite everything, she was the one who had stood up for him throughout the years. But he worried that the truth would make her even sicker.

"I'm… I'm gay, mom. Dad found out. The way he spoke to me at the store after… I can't stay here anymore, not after that. I'll explain everything later, but now I just have to leave, okay?"

Jake retraced his steps back up the stairs and kissed his mother on the cheek. She was looking at him, open mouthed and in shock, but Jake only turned around and carried on down the stairs. He looked up before opening the front door, though, and saw his mother now grabbing the handrail hard, sobbing silently.

CHAPTER 8

THE DRIZZLE MUTED the colors and blurred the houses. Jake stood for a moment on the curb, looking around, feeling cold droplets of rain on his skin. It almost felt like being inside a very thick coat of mist, like that one time he went climbing and realized the clouds he saw at a distance were more like fog up close. Jake pulled his hoodie forward and crossed the street.

He had left his parent's house without looking back, afraid he would otherwise not be able to leave his mother, what with her crying like that. It was just temporary, though. He wasn't abandoning her, right? He just needed to get as far away from his father as possible and find the time to think about what to do next. But was he being self-centered or, worse, selfish? Shouldn't he be able to bite his lip and take his father's crap? Didn't his mother at least deserve that? She did. But Jake had reached his limit and the last thing he wanted was for her to see him beating the crap out of the old man. Right now he only knew one thing: he wouldn't take any more shit from him.

Jake hurriedly crossed the street to the porch where he shook his duffel bag, trying to clear some of the water now starting to soak his clothes but only managing to dampen them even more. He pulled the hoodie back and combed his hair with his fingers. Jake knew he was only stalling, making excuses to postpone ringing the bell. He wasn't sure he was doing the right thing or that he would be welcomed. It was one thing being received with open arms and going for a bite to eat but this would be an entirely different proposition.

He took a deep breath and rang the bell. The only noises around him were the water droplets falling from the roof and the occasional car passing by.

The door opened. "I was just thinking of you," Britta said, welcoming him with her big smile, but one that vanished when she saw his face. "What happened to you?"

Jake touched his jaw instinctively. "It's nothing, don't worry. I'm sorry to drop by without calling first, but I kinda need your help. Can I come in?"

Britta's gaze fell on his duffel bag and travelled back to his eyes. "Of course. Is everything okay?" she said, taking a step back and opening the door for him.

"Not really," he said as he entered the house. Jake placed his bag on the floor and put his hands in his jean's pockets. Britta closed the door behind them.

"I know this is unexpected, but I kinda needed a place to crash in for a while."

"Oh, my goodness. Did you father kick you out?"

Jake sighed. "Not exactly, but I left. He found out I was gay and we had a huge fight. He said horrible things. I couldn't stay in my old house after that."

"Aww, Jake. I'm so sorry," she said. Britta approached him and leaned in to give him a hug, but Jake stopped her.

"I'm soaking wet," he said.

"Don't be silly. It's just water. Come here."

Britta held him in a tender embrace. Jake stiffened a bit but was soon melting within that warm hug, letting himself be surrounded by her affection. He lay his head on Britta's shoulder and cried. It hadn't been planned. He didn't even know he was going to. It just happened when he realized he hadn't lost much because he had never had it in the first place. So he cried for himself and for the lack of love he had always felt in his own home.

A couple of minutes later, Britta went to fetch a towel for Jake to dry some of the water on his clothes.

"How did your father find out about you?" she asked.

Jake stopped drying himself with the towel but didn't face her immediately. After a moment looking at his own shoes, he looked up.

"Almost a year ago, I made a terrible mistake. I started dating this guy, Hunter. It was the worst thing I did in my life. He was at the store today and told my father everything. Next thing I know, he was screaming at me that I was an abomination and then he hit me."

Britta gasped and covered her mouth. "Oh my goodness. Are you okay?" she asked, approaching his face, looking for bruises.

"I'm alright. He didn't hit me that hard."

"Why didn't you tell me you had a boyfriend?"

"I don't. I ran from him a week ago and came here…"

Britta blinked several times and raised her eyebrows. "You ran from him?"

"He was a mistake. A big one. Hunter was cute and flattering, and told me everything I wanted to hear: that I was beautiful, that I made him happy, that I deserved someone that made me feel like a prince… I fell for that and, next thing I know, he was showing me a side of him that wasn't that pretty." Jake paused.

"Did he cheat on you?"

"No…"

"What, then? You're making me nervous!"

"He's … aggressive. When things don't go his way, he can be scary. So, I ended up doing everything I could to please him just so the night wouldn't end up with him screaming at me."

"Oh, my God, Jake. Did he beat you?"

"Once he almost did but he only pushed me to the bed in the end."

"Oh, honey. Why didn't you leave him sooner?"

Jake's eyes filled with tears. He cleaned them with the back of his hand. "Because he was controlling and I had to tell him everywhere I went. He was constantly texting me and one time I think he even put someone after me just to make sure I wasn't cheating on him or something. I got afraid of what he could do. " Jake paused again, sniffed and sighed loudly. "Last week I mustered up the courage to leave him and ran away. I only took what I could and left. I even ditched my old cell phone before coming here."

"My God, Jake. It sounds like something out of a movie," Britta said, shaking her head. "But how did he find you?"

"He saw where I was on Matt's phone, a friend of mine. He texted and warned me that night I came to have dinner here."

Britta's eyes opened wide. "So that's why you went pale. Why didn't you say something? We could've helped you."

"I was embarrassed and we had just met after all these years… I guess I was afraid of what you might think."

"Don't be silly. We need to do something about that Hunter. How about we go to the police?"

Jake scoffed. "I can't go to the police. What would I tell them? My boyfriend is violent and might hit me? I don't have any proof and honestly I don't feel comfortable going to them."

"Why not?"

Why not indeed. Jake's mind raced to find an answer. He had said it, and he knew from the minute Britta had suggested going to the police that he didn't feel comfortable with it, but he didn't know why. And then it hit him. He didn't want them to think he was a sissy. Jake saw himself as a man. A gay man, but a man nonetheless. Going to the police and asking for help because of his boyfriend? That'd make him a sissy.

"I don't think it's necessary," he ended up saying. "Now that I have your help I think I'll be able to tell him to get lost." Jake smiled but felt embarrassed by his own thoughts.

"Well, let's not think of that, then. I'll prepare the guest bedroom for you."

An overwhelming sense of relief took over Jake. "Thanks for letting me stay."

"You're welcome, honey. Don't worry about it. You can stay as long as you want."

"You sure it's okay? Your husband won't mind?"

Britta's eyes became overshadowed by a glaze of pain. It only lasted a moment and then her usual smile was back on her face. "Don't worry about him. It's fine. Come. I'll show you where the bedroom is. You can get those wet clothes off while I prepare you a shower. We don't want you catching a cold or something."

CHAPTER 9

JAKE SPENT THE rest of the day in the bedroom Britta had so kindly prepared for him. He felt a need to curl himself up in a ball and sleep, to close the bedroom door and the window curtains and just feel the bed sheets beneath him, concentrate on that cottony feeling, and forget about his father and his life. That dread that sometimes appeared out of nowhere and paralyzed him was now nibbling on his toes, spreading through his legs, into his gut and chest, making him cold inside. There was a part of him that kept saying that everything would be fine, that he wasn't all alone in the world. He had his mother and Britta. And even Craig. Jake rolled on the bed. Craig's disheartened face, when he'd heard Hunter at the store, kept appearing to him, and every time it did he felt his gut clenching. But he was sure Craig would come around after he'd explained who Hunter was. Or maybe there wasn't anything to explain and Craig wasn't even thinking of him. Maybe his expression had just been from his own awkwardness at the whole situation in the store. Jake rolled on the bed again and covered his head with the duvet. Maybe if he stayed still enough that dread that threatened to consume him from his insides would go away.

When he didn't leave the room that night to have dinner, Britta brought him a sandwich.

"Get some sleep. Tomorrow everything will seem better. You'll see," she said.

***

Jake woke up the next day with a sunbeam pressing on his eyelids. The light had found a way through a small misaligned patch of fabric in the curtains. He stretched himself and looked around, not knowing where he was. His brain still seemed to be sleeping and he had no idea which room he was in or why he wasn't in his attic.

You're an abomination!

The memory of the previous day rushed to fill every corner of his mind, overwhelming him with a nasty feeling. Suddenly, the stillness of the room made him feel sick. He felt like a traitor for abandoning his mother at a time when she needed him the most.

Jake looked at his phone. It was almost noon. He jumped out of bed and rushed to the bathroom to wash his face and brush his teeth. He had to go see his mother, explain everything to her and tell her that, although he didn't live there anymore, he wasn't abandoning her.

He left the house running, without eating breakfast or taking a shower. Fifteen minutes later, he was ringing the doorbell at his parent's house. He waited for his mother to open the door, shifting his bodyweight from foot to foot, nervous how she'd react. He didn't have to wonder for long, though, for the door soon opened. His mother stood there, looking at him, her eyes filling with tears.

Jake opened his mouth to apologize, to say he was sorry for everything, although he wasn't quite sure what he wanted to apologize for. Him not being the perfect son his mother had imagined? An abomination in the eyes of their God? He couldn't speak, though. A knot had settled in his throat, a big mess of feelings bubbling up in his chest, waiting to explode. But he couldn't cry. He wouldn't. Not this time. He wasn't ashamed anymore. He didn't want to be. The only thing he regretted was having a redneck of a father who wasn't able to support his mother like she deserved.

"Can I come in?" he managed to say in a faint voice.

His mother didn't reply but hugged him, sobbing silently. Despite her illness, he felt all of her strength in that embrace.

"Please don't cry."

His mother took a step back and cleared her tears. "How can I do that when I feel like I lost you, Jake?"

"You haven't, mom. I'm here for you. Just as before."

"Did I do something to put you on this road? Was it me? Am I to blame?"

Jake felt his gut twitching. "No, mom, it's not your fault. It's not anyone's fault. I'm just like this. It's who I am."

His mother sighed deeply and went inside. Jake followed her in, closing the door behind him.

"But it's a sin, Jake. You know what the Bible says about homosexuals."

"The Bible says lots of things; it's wrong to be left handed, it's wrong to eat shrimp, it's wrong to eat pork… Women who get divorced should be stoned to death. I don't see that many people worrying about those. They seem to pick and choose what they want to follow as a truth. I'm a good person, mom. This is just a part of who I am."

"What if you just haven't met the right girl? Maybe it's just a matter of time. How can you be certain you won't change your mind later on?" she asked, worry creases marring her forehead.

"Mom, I'm not going to change. It doesn't work that way. This is not a choice or a lifestyle. I didn't choose to be gay as I didn't choose to have blond hair. I'm not going to change, mom. I can't."

His mother dropped her head and locked eyes with her thumbs. "I'm so scared God will punish you, Jake."

"He already has, mom. Dad is making sure of it."

"Your father only wants what's best for you."

Jake sighed. "Dad hates me."

She looked up, wide-eyed and shaking her head. "Don't say that, it's not true, Jake."

"If you saw how he treated me yesterday, you wouldn't be saying that. Dad hates me, mom. He always has." Jake paced the room, looking at the walls. "Yesterday he told me he'd always known I was different, that I had the devil inside of me, that I was effeminate and that's why he used to beat me." He stopped pacing and looked down, scoffing. "He just wanted to beat the devil out of me—these are his own words—but apparently, he couldn't. You should have seen the look on his face."

His mother coughed and Jake turned around. Her skin was now a little grey. He hurried to her side and grabbed her arm, helping her sit down on the couch.

"Forget about dad," he said. "I'm here because I'm worried about you, not because of him. Is he helping you?"

His mother sighed. "You know how your father is…"

They both sat in silence for a couple of minutes, contemplating their own thoughts.

"When's your next treatment?"

His mother observed him. "Thursday."

"I want to go with you."

"There's no need, Jake. I can ask Bette to go with me."

"I want to spend time with you. It's one of the reasons I came back."

His mother pursed her lips. "Okay, but don't tell your father. He's very upset right now."

"I don't intend to talk to—"

The front door opened and they both turned their heads. Jake's father stood in the doorframe, a frown covering his face.

"What the hell is he doing here?"

"Steve, please—"

"The nerve of you to come here, after what you've done. Don't you have any shame? Don't you know what you're doing to your mother?!" he shouted, as he entered the room.

Jake got up, his insides burning with anger. He just wanted to punch this awful man. Instead, he approached his mother and kissed her on the forehead.

"Bye, mom."

As he walked past, his father grabbed Jake's arm.

"Don't you ever come here again. I'm changing the locks. I don't want you coming in whenever you want. This is a house of God. You're not welcome here." His tone was low and menacing. Jake yanked his arm from his grip, panting and trying hard not to punch the man in the face. He fought back tears that insisted on being noticed and left the house. After all, he had to think of his mother's health.

CHAPTER 10

THE NEXT DAY, Jake woke up feeling oddly rested. He had this feeling that he'd dreamt something last night, something that was utterly enjoyable and that filled him to the brim with a warm feeling. He stretched himself and turned his head to the window and the heavy curtains that hid the world outside. The light that seeped through was bright. Jake wondered if the day would be sunny. He was completely sick and tired of the rain. He got up from the bed, approached the window and opened the curtains. He blinked a couple of times. The light was bright, yes, but only compared to the previous darkness of the room. The sky was still covered in a fluffy mantle of clouds.

He went to the bathroom, smiling. He didn't care about the weather. Somehow, whatever it was he'd dreamt had dislodged that emptiness that clung to him after he'd walked away from his parent's house. Jake looked in the mirror, recalling his father's words when he'd arrived at the house, and shook his head. His father was a really sick person, only happy when he was spilling bile over other people, judging them, scaring them with the fires of hell.

As he brought the toothbrush to his mouth, he realized his father's words didn't have any power over him anymore. *Damn. That must've been a really good dream.* And then, something struck him, something he should have thought of years ago: his father was probably utterly unhappy. He remembered seeing him in church, shivering before the minister every time he spoke about the punishment God would serve to those who didn't abide by his laws. Afterwards, his father would look around and make snide comments about those who weren't as scared as he obviously was. What a sad life that was, always scared of an invisible being hovering over you, watching your every move and thought.

He rinsed out his mouth and left the bathroom. He just hoped his mother realized that he was still the same Jake, that everything was the same. She just knew him better now, that was all. Unfortunately, he hadn't had the chance to end their talk properly.

Jake went downstairs, his stomach growling. He called for Britta but she wasn't home, so he went into the kitchen and prepared himself a sandwich. There was a note on the counter saying she had gone grocery shopping.

He finished his sandwich and went upstairs again to take a shower. His life was a mess, sure, but things would get better. In the bathroom, he turned on the shower while he undressed himself, and Craig popped into his mind. He wondered how he'd gotten to go out to his parents and what their reaction had been. Judging by how happy Craig now appeared to be, though, it must've been a thousand times better than his own experience.

He entered the shower, trying to think of what to do next with his life. The hot water helped him focus, and the more he thought about it, the more he wanted to spend time with his mother. No matter how hard his father tried he wouldn't let the man's bitterness consume him. And his father most certainly wouldn't get in the way of Jake spending time with his mother.

Jake closed the water off and took a fluffy towel from the rack. He was drying himself off when the doorbell rang. He thought to ignore it but whoever was there didn't seem too keen on giving up. When the doorbell rang a fourth time, he took a deep breath and wrapped the towel around his waist. He went downstairs, grabbing the towel with one hand, afraid it might fall off at the worst possible moment. He crossed the living room and noticed it had started raining.

"Craig?" he said, after opening the door.

Craig stared at him for a moment, wet from the rain. He had what seemed to be a shocked expression, like Jake was the last person on earth he expected to see here. And he probably was.

"What are you doing here? Where's Britta?" he asked at the same time as his eyes ran Jake from head to toe.

Jake never felt more naked. He could see Craig's eyes examining him and wished he had spent more time at the gym. Jake gripped his towel tighter. "She went grocery shopping. Want to come in? It's a bit chilly out there." Jake could feel his nipples hardening from the cold air invading the living room.

"Sure," Craig said, entering the house.

"Do you want me to get you a towel? You're all wet." As he'd said this, Jake had noticed that Craig's wet jeans seemed to accentuate even more his bubble butt. Jake's dick jumped at the thought and he felt a wave of embarrassment taking him over. *Really? After all that's happened you're getting a boner?* He just hoped the folds of the towel were enough to disguise his growing hard-on.

"No, thanks. I'm fine. Do you know if Britta's going to take long?"

Craig moved with the confidence of a proper man. "No clue." Jake fought not to look at Craig's crotch but couldn't help himself. He was already imagining what lurked beneath all that soaked fabric that revealed such a very interesting shape. You could tell the man was worth exploring with your bare hands and Jake imagined just how big his cock had to be to produce that kind of bulge. He felt his own dick jumping again at the thought. His eyes traveled up again and he forced himself not to look at Craig's crotch. "Do you want some coffee? Have you eaten already?"

Craig was slightly flushed and Jake couldn't tell if it was out of embarrassment or from the contrast between the outside cold and the warmth in the living room. "No, thanks. I'm good. I... I'd better go. Could you tell Britta I was here? I'll call her anyway," Craig said, walking towards the front door.

"Listen," Jake blurted, grabbing Craig's arm instinctively as he walked by. He let go immediately, like he had been burned by a hot piece of ember. Craig stopped and turned to Jake. "About the other day... I'm sorry about that incident at my father's store and Hunter. I just wanted to tell you that he's crazy and what he said is not true. He's not my boyfriend. Well, not anymore anyway. If you still want to, I'd like to have that drink with you sometime."

Craig's eyes were jumping all over Jake. "Look, it seems to me that you two still have issues to deal with. Maybe we can have a drink when you have it all sorted out. We all have our messy pasts to deal with, but I'm not looking for complicated stuff right now."

"Hunter was a mistake I'm still paying for. I want to distance myself from him. He's manipulative and aggressive and I should never have fallen for him. But that's all in the past, Craig. He's one of the reasons I came back. I was running from him." Jake sighed. "I understand if this is too much for you but I just wanted to tell you that we're not together anymore."

Craig's eyes had widened as Jake spoke and a patch of wrinkles appeared on his forehead as he quirked his eyebrows. He seemed surprised, like he'd expected anything but that story.

"Did he beat you?" he asked, approaching Jake, his eyes sweeping him like he was searching for clues of mistreatment.

Jake felt Craig's body heat and his heart raced as he realized Craig was probably worried about him. "No, never."

Craig seemed to notice Jake's flushed face and took a step back. He turned his head away, looked at the door and opened and closed his mouth a couple of times, before saying: "So, you're not seeing him anymore?" A smile was already forcing itself onto his face.

Jake shook his head.

"Then I guess there's no reason why we couldn't have a drink tonight. What do you say?"

"Tonight sounds perfect," he said, making an effort not to giggle like an idiot. He didn't know where that had come from.

"It's a date, then. I'll see you later," Craig said, smiling. He turned for the door and left.

Jake stood still, staring at the doorway and hearing his own heartbeat. He noticed a pressure in his crotch and realized that what had been a growing hard-on was now a raging boner, impossible to ignore. He ran upstairs to the guest bedroom. As he entered the private bathroom, he took the towel off and went into the shower again. He needed to unload that excess of energy Craig had gotten into him. His dick throbbed in anticipation, as big as he'd ever seen it, asking to be touched. He lubed his hand with a bit of water and started stroking it with hard, strong movements, pumping it ever faster, until it almost hurt. He could already feel the pressure increasing as he brushed the head of his cock, his slippery hand shooting electric jolts deep inside of him. Jake had not realized how aroused he was, how Craig had made his cock so hard and in need of closure. He recalled Craig's bulge in his wet pants, imagining a big, veiny cock beneath the fabric, just asking to be sucked. He couldn't take it anymore. His muscles tensed up and he shot his load, gushing it all over the shower. It was like his dick was a fire hose trying to extinguish the fire that was burning him up. Jake let a cry out, breathing raggedly as the spasms made his dick spit its final drops of cum.

He panted for a minute, trying to catch his breath and feeling alive for the first time in weeks, like he'd just woken up from a bad dream and was suddenly able to feel the world around him once more.

CHAPTER 11

WHEN BRITTA ARRIVED home, Jake was already downstairs and on the couch, looking at the window without really seeing it. He was lost in thought, reviewing what he'd been through in the last few days. It all made him feel like he'd lived for a lifetime in only a week. And although his current situation sucked, he felt alive, like he was starting to gain control over his life and finally standing up to the paralyzing fear that had been with him for so long.

He smiled to himself, recalling the urgency he'd felt because of Craig, imagining what could be beneath his clothes. Two weeks ago he couldn't have imagined he'd be here, his high school crush for Craig fuelling his desire once again.

"Hey, honey. Did you see my note?" Britta said, entering the living room with two bags full of groceries. Jake turned to her, startled. His mind had been so far away he'd not heard her come in. Britta chuckled. "I'm sorry. Didn't mean to scare you."

"I didn't hear you arrive. Let me help you with that," Jake said, getting up from the couch. He approached Britta and helped her with the bags. "Craig dropped by. He was looking for you," he said as they went into the kitchen.

"Did he say what he wanted?"

"No, only that he'd call you."

"That's odd. I didn't receive any phone call."

Jake placed the bags on the kitchen counter, trying to curb a giggle that insisted on being noted. Britta must've notice something, though, because she looked at him with her head on one side.

"Is there something wrong? Why are you making that face?" she asked, while putting the groceries in the cabinet.

"Craig asked me out for a drink," he said, grinning.

Britta stopped what she was doing and turned to Jake. "He did? My word. You boys are so fast on these things. I mean, the other day you were in my living room, crying because of Hunter. I wouldn't be able to go out on a date with something like that on my mind."

Jake's smile vanished. Suddenly, his happiness was again under siege by his problems, he could almost feel their spikes trying to pierce his warm and fuzzy bubble. "I'm just trying to make the best out of this horrible situation," he said, a bit hurt. "Do you think I shouldn't go out with him?" Maybe Britta was right. Maybe he should be focusing on finding a solution to Hunter.

"I'm not saying that. I'm just saying I, personally, would be worried sick because of Hunter. That's all."

Jake observed Britta as she stored the groceries away. "Well, you know, I've decided not to give in to fear anymore," he said, his gaze locked on the counter while he drew imaginary shapes there with his fingers. "I know I have crazy Hunter after me, and my crazy father, who hates me, to deal with, but I just thought I could put all that aside for a moment and try to be happy. This past year has been terrible and I've developed these… I don't know what to call them. It's like I feel my limbs getting colder and a paralyzing fear taking over. I don't want that anymore. I want to be in control of my life."

"I'm sorry, honey. I didn't mean to judge you. Who am I to do that, anyway?" Britta's smile was nowhere to be seen. She seemed unhappy.

"Is everything okay?" Jake asked, approaching her after a moment of silence.

Britta continued putting things into the cabinets. "Yeah, everything's fine."

"Britta, please look at me. What's wrong? I can tell something's the matter." Britta's shoulders dropped and she started sobbing. Jake hugged her and for a minute said nothing.

"It's Eric, my husband... He isn't coming home."

Jake knew there was something off with Britta and her husband since the night they were supposed to have dinner together. He let her cry for a while, feeling her tremble in his arms, shaken by occasional sobs. He could feel her pain.

When the sobs subsided, Jake asked: "Is he travelling or something? What happened?"

Britta lifted her head from his shoulder. Her eyes were all puffy and smudged from her mascara. "He said he's met someone, that he has to think about us because he was confused..."

"What? Confused? That's bullshit!" Jake said, feeling angry for the man's terrible excuse and immediately regretting his outburst. He didn't want to hurt Britta even more. "I'm sorry. I shouldn't have said—"

"No, it's fine. You're right," she said, pulling Jake by his arm towards the kitchen stools. They sat and she sighed. "It is bullshit. We were going through a rough patch, yes, but what the fuck is up just giving up on someone you were supposed to love?" Britta was red and wide-eyed. As soon as she noticed her phrasing, though, she covered her mouth with her hands. "I'm sorry. I swore. I don't swear." She seemed embarrassed and surprised at the same time.

Jake smiled. "I think it's the least you can do, given the circumstances."

"You know what bothers me the most? I gave that man three years of my life. I gave up college and Europe for him. I was supposed to go to Europe for a semester? Remember? Those were my grandiose plans, anyway... And this is how he repays me. He's confused?" Britta scoffed. "Well fuck him, that's what." Britta's pain was quickly transforming into anger. Once again she covered her mouth as soon as she realized what she'd said. "I know the decision was mine, but I gave up college for him and gave him nothing but affection. And then he does this to me? You must think I'm a very stupid woman," Britta said, using a paper tissue to clean away the fresh tears that had filled her eyes.

"Don't say that. You're not stupid, you're just a sweet, hopeless romantic."

Britta exhaled sharply, a mixture of a sob and a failed laugh. "And see what that did for me: I'm a housewife stuck in a small town in the middle of nowhere, smiling everywhere I go because I'm too ashamed to admit I made a huge mistake."

Jake hugged Britta. "We all make mistakes. You don't have to be ashamed of them. Have I told you about my life?" he said, trying to lighten the mood. "Just try to pick a better man next time, okay?"

"I'm so glad you're back in town. I don't have any real friends here," she said, between sobs.

Jake leaned back, held Britta by her shoulders and looked deeply into her eyes. "I propose we make a pact, right here and now. From now on, we're going to start the process of taking hold of our own destiny. To hell with letting others hurt us and making us feel less than we are. No more of going with the flow, of having others decide for us what we should do. What do you say? Shall we be the captains of our own fate?"

Britta smiled while a fat tear ran down her face. "That's the best damn thing anyone's told me in the last couple of years."

CHAPTER 12

THE COLD AIR brushed Jake's ears and raised the hairs at the nape of his neck. He felt a shiver run down his spine and he pulled his jacket closer. The night was freezing. He crossed the street at a brisk pace. In front of him was Buddha, one of the very few bars the town had and the place where Craig had suggested they meet. Jake had agreed on the spot because he knew nothing about going out in his old town. Heck, he didn't even know you could go on a night out in this excuse of a town, not on a week day. When he'd left, they'd only had a big shopping mall and a couple of old bars, the kind you didn't want to be in after a certain hour.

According to Britta, Buddha had changed names and gone through renovations recently, and it showed. Upon arriving, Jake noticed how modern it looked, with its blue and silver tones, straight lines and expansive use of glass. Far too fancy for a small town like this.

Jake scanned the place, trying to find Craig. He was nowhere to be seen so he went to the counter. The bartender seemed a bit bored and was watching TV. As he approached, Jake thought this would be a nice place to take Britta, to get her mind off her problems. He had insisted on staying home to keep her company, but she'd refused. She said there was no good in Jake staying in if he had a chance at getting it on. Britta had laughed and Jake knew this was her way of trying to be funny and to show him she'd be okay.

"Can I have a beer, please?" He looked at his watch. 9 p.m., like they had agreed. Was it too soon? Was he supposed to arrive fashionably late?

"Hey there, stranger. May I join you?"

Someone tapped Jake's back in a friendly manner. He turned around and saw Craig grinning, his brown-green eyes piercing Jake to his soul.

Jake smiled back. "Hey. I've just arrived. Do you want a beer?"

"Sure." Craig grabbed his wallet from his jacket.

"No, no. There's no need for that," Jake said, shaking his head.

"Let me pay for the beers and you can buy the next round."

Craig's eyes were deep and his voice deeper still. He was oozing charisma and Jake didn't know how to say no. "Okay, thanks."

The barman gave them their beers and Craig raised his bottle. "Cheers," he said.

"Cheers," Jake returned, unable to contain a grin.

"Wanna go sit at a table?"

They left the counter and went to a corner, to sit at one of the many tables available. Buddha wasn't exactly crowded. Jake took a sip of his beer and smiled at Craig, not knowing what to say. Craig did the same. It was definitely weird being here with him. Jake had dreamt about it in his teen years. Well, at least he'd dreamt of something similar as, back then, the town didn't have fancy bars.

"So, here we are," Jake finally said, trying to break the ice.

"Here we are…"

They weren't going anywhere like this.

"How's your father?" Jake ventured.

"He's doing okay, given the circumstances. I've been trying to get him out of the house and have him do something other than sit around and look out the window, but it's not easy."

"I'm sorry about your mother." Jake felt a sudden need to hug Craig and comfort him.

"Thanks. Can we change the subject, though?" he said, crinkling his eyes. "I'm feeling guilty as it is for leaving my father alone for the evening."

Jake now realized the subject was far from being sexy. "I'm sorry. I was just trying to make conversation. I suck at this."

Craig smiled. "Is that why you ended up with that douche bag that was at your father's store?"

Jake's face heated up. "Probably. I just have the worst taste in men." He felt embarrassed as soon as he finished the sentence. He wanted to show he was interested in Craig, but didn't want him to think he was talking about him.

"Are you trying to imply something?" Craig said, his eyes narrowing on Jake, a warm smile across his face.

Jake smiled back and tried to breathe. "I didn't say I was interested in you, did I?"

Craig opened his mouth to reply but laughed instead. "Well, touché, sir."

Jake felt better, like someone had lifted a weight from his shoulders and the conversation began to flow. They talked about life after leaving town and Craig told him he was now a 3D artist in San Francisco. His job involved creating images on a computer that could be sold as photos for catalogues, or for architects and real estate agencies that wanted to sell houses before they were built. Although he had had his fair share of boyfriends, he'd got fed up with the drama and the shallowness of most of them. By the third beer, Jake was telling Craig about his dream of being a writer and that he'd left his father's store.

"You left the store?"

"Well, after being slapped in the face by my father and listening to him calling me a sinner, I realized I'd had enough."

"He hit you?" Craig reached his hand to Jake's face. It was obvious he was just acting out of concern, instinctively trying to see if Jake was hurt, but Jake could only think of that hand on his face; that big, warm hand, touching him and making his head spin. His heart had jumped at the touch and his ears were now filled with the sound of blood pumping. Jake tilted his head ever so slightly, embracing Craig's touch, and closed his eyes for a moment. When he realized what he was doing, he moved away and blushed.

"It's okay, really. I barely registered the slap. Anyway, I left the store and moved out of the house. That's actually why you saw me this morning at Britta's. I'm staying with her while I sort things out."

Craig smiled and looked deeply into his eyes. "I'm really glad we ran into each other," he said. "I have a confession to make. I… I had a crush on you in high school, you know? I never told you that. I felt too embarrassed back then to admit it. You seemed so different from all the other kids…"

The thumping on Jake's ribcage increased. He couldn't believe what he was hearing. He wanted to giggle and squeal, and tell the whole world that Craig Mathews had a crush on him; or used to. Instead, he let himself grin, after a deep breath taken in as silently as possible. "You thought I was different? That was because I was a closeted gay who didn't know what being gay meant. On top of it, I was such a geek!" He'd felt too embarrassed to address the part where Craig had confessed his own crush. *Why did you change the subject? He used to like you! Focus on that, you idiot!*

Craig chuckled. "Well, if by geek you mean someone intelligent, then yes, you were. I distinctively remember you being one of the brightest in class."

Jake's heartbeat was now a runaway train and he could feel his ears burning up.

"I don't know about that. But there were lots of cuter guys in school. Josh! You remember Josh? He was cute. And hot." Jake regretted immediately what he'd said and pressed his lips together. *Why are you saying that? Tell him he was the cute one. Not Josh!*

"Josh? He was not! Way too muscular. I was always afraid one of his veins was going to pop or something," Craig said, laughing. "You have a thing for strong men, do you?"

"Not all men. Just the right ones." Jake felt the beer messing with his brain. *Oh, my god, Jake. What the hell are you doing? Could you be more cheesy?* He decided to cut the crap. "I'm sorry. I don't know why I'm trying to be flirty. It's obviously not my thing. I guess it's because I also had a crush on you back in high school and now you've told me about yours and I'm nervous."

Craig smiled and his eyes locked with Jake's, probing the darkest recesses of his soul. He leaned forward and kissed Jake, gently. It was just a hint of a kiss, his lips brushing tenderly on Jake's. The soft touch triggered a heatwave throughout Jake's body, which concentrated itself in his crotch. His head spun like he had had too much to drink and his mind overflowed with thoughts. In the midst of them, there was one that kept coming back: *Craig is kissing me! This is really happening!*

After a moment, Craig leaned back, his gaze scanning Jake like he was searching for some kind of refuge. Jake opened his eyes, panting and flushed, his heartbeat drumming in his ears. Craig leaned forward again and kissed him. This time, the kiss was firm, his lips pressing against Jake's with unyielding resolve. Any thoughts of fear for being in a small-town bar kissing another man quickly vanished from Jake's mind as his heart pounded in his ribcage and his skin hummed with pleasure.

Craig leaned back again, smiling. Jake smiled back, all flushed, his chest bursting with joy. He couldn't remember a time when he'd felt happier than right now.

"I'm sorry, I don't want to, but I should go," Craig said, looking down at his watch. "I promised my dad I wouldn't be long, but I'd like to see you again."

Jake's smile extinguished itself for a second, like a candle exposed to a draft. He felt disappointed that their night had to end, but it was so endearing to see Craig worried about his father that there was no way he could feel mad at him. A grin forced itself onto his face. "I'd love to see you again, too."

"Can I give you a ride back to Britta's?"

Jake looked out through the windows of the bar, the rain splattered across their glass. "Well, after much deliberation I say you can. I've thought about it and I'm not in the mood for getting soaking wet."

Craig laughed. They got up and walked to the exit. Jake had a silly smile on his face that refused to go away. When they got outside, it wasn't raining; it was pouring. Craig dashed to his car and Jake followed. The man sure could run fast. They jumped in the car and sat in silence for a minute, panting and drenched, trying to catch their breath. Jake stole a peek at Craig. Although it was dark, he remembered how the clothes had hugged him earlier that morning, making the bulge in his jeans stand out even more. Jake's dick jumped at this thought and he felt embarrassed. Craig had caught Jake stealing the peek. Their eyes met and Jake felt an electric jolt run through his spine, concentrating itself on his cock. Before he knew it, he'd leaned forward and kissed Craig. He had to feel his lips one last time, those tender, full, and oh, so sweet lips, before Craig went home to his dad. Craig kissed him back and grabbed him by his neck with an urgency that made Jake moan with desire.

Jake grabbed Craig's cock through his jeans, feeling it for the first time. God, it was stiff and there was much more to it that he'd thought. It was a real handful. His own dick throbbed, jolts of lust running through it.

"Please stop," Craig whispered a second later, his hand on top of Jake's. "I really want this but I have to go. I'm worried about my father. I'm sorry."

Jake could see how aroused Craig was from his panting and was undecided between being frustrated or charmed by Craig's sense of responsibility. "It's okay. I understand," he said, leaning back to his seat and trying to control his own fast breathing.

Craig's gaze perused him one last time and he started the car, driving away from the bar's parking lot. Even in the dim light, Jake could see his face was red and his eyes hungry.

"I'll make it up to you, I promise," Craig said a minute later.

Jake felt Craig's hand searching for his and holding it tightly, resting afterwards on top of his leg. "You don't have to. It's not like you did something wrong," he said, trying to ignore his raging hard-on. It was the right thing to do, though. Craig was a decent guy and he didn't want to make him feel guilty for caring about his father.

Craig drove in silence for a couple of minutes, his hand holding Jake's. "I know I've said it before, but I'm really glad we met again." He glanced at Jake, grinning, before his gaze returned to the road.

"Me too," Jake said, feeling Craig squeeze his hand a bit more.

They passed by Britta's house, Craig not stopping.

"Britta's back there," he said, turning to Craig.

"I know." He was grinning and his voice was deep. He followed the road and stopped the car after turning into a narrow road, far away from the main street.

"What are we doing here?" Jake asked, as Craig turned off the car.

"I think my father can wait a bit longer," Craig said, his voice hoarse with desire. He leaned in, brushing Jake's lips softly with his own, turning his insides into molten lava. Craig grabbed his neck and pressed harder, kissing him feverishly, parting his lips with his tongue. Jake returned his kiss, panting and feeling Craig's beard, his dick throbbing and alive with a mind of its own.

Craig ran his strong hand down Jake's torso and stopped at his crotch, his hand exploring the shapes beneath the fabric. He stroked Jake's now rock-hard cock through his pants and, with determined movements, unbuttoned Jake's jeans, panting, trying to undo his own as fast as he could. Jake's mind swirled with flashes of fleeting thoughts, having a hard time believing this was actually happening. Craig pulled Jake's jeans down and freed his cock from his boxer shorts. He leaned over and put Jake's dick in his mouth, exploring it with his tongue and then sucking it, bobbing with renewed need. Jake felt himself disappearing inside Craig's mouth, a moist embrace that turned him inside out when he felt his cock's head brushing against Craig's throat.

I don't believe this is happening. "Please stop or I'm gonna come!" Jake managed to say between heavily drawn breaths.

Craig bobbed and sucked even faster and Jake felt himself being pulled into an abyss of pleasure, a mounting pressure deep inside from which there was no turning back. A second later and Jake cried as his body shivered with spasms and he emptied his load, feeling an ecstasy he couldn't ever remember feeling before.

Jake's mind wandered for a second, high on endorphins. He could only hear his own heart racing, threatening to break free of his ribcage. A moment later, the world started to become focused again as he came down from the blissful heaven in which he'd been engulfed. He opened his eyes and his gaze fell on Craig. He smiled and caressed his face. Craig held Jake's hand and kissed it. Then he started the car.

"Wait," Jake said, covering Craig's hand with his own. "How about you?"

Craig chuckled. "This isn't a competition, silly. You'll get your chance." A broad grin set itself on Craig's face as he drove them away.

CHAPTER 13

CRAIG STOPPED IN front of Britta's house. "This is you," he said in a low voice, turning his head to Jake and making his insides shudder. His voice was so manly Jake could spend all night listening to him talk.

"I loved tonight. I couldn't be happier." He'd said it with a silly, wide grin on his face. But he couldn't avoid it. He was *that* happy.

Craig leaned in and kissed him and Jake's dick again jumped to life. He moved back.

"You better go," Jake said, the corner of his lips all the way up. "Someone is waking up downstairs and I can't answer for him."

Craig burst into laughter. "You address your dick as *him*? Do you also have a name for it?"

"Shut up."

"Oh, my god. You totally do."

"Even if I did, now I'm not telling you," Jake said, crossing his arms.

"Maybe next time?" Craig winked.

"We'll see about that."

Jake got out of the car. The rain had stopped. He stood on the curb and watched Craig leave, waiting until his car's red lights disappeared down the intersection. He sighed and turned around to go into the house. He didn't want the night to end. He just wanted that happy feeling to linger for as long as possible.

An approaching shadow caught his eye. He turned his head instinctively and saw Hunter crossing the street in long strides. He was tall, at almost six feet three, and had no trouble walking really fast. Jake's heart jumped and his stomach sank. He felt the blood fleeing from his face and a dull pain in his temples.

"Come with me. This has gone far enough," Hunter simply said, cutting off Jake's escape. His voice was determined and Jake noted a hint of anger in his squarish face. Hunter had always reminded him of a younger Jason Statham, on account of his solid frame.

"What are you doing here? Are you following me?" Jake asked, looking up at him. His voice had come out in a higher pitch than he'd intended.

Hunter sighed. "I'm getting really annoyed with all this bullshit, Jake. Just get in the car and let's go. You've made me waste enough time as it is."

The blood that had fled Jake's face now surged to his cheeks. "I'm not going anywhere. Leave me alone." Jake took a step forward, trying to get around Hunter, but he cut his path off again.

"Get in the car!" Hunter hissed, grabbing Jake's forearm. His eyes were two menacing slits. Jake had forgotten how strong he was, but was now reminded of it.

Jake yanked his arm free. His heart pounded. He knew that look and was scared Hunter would do something crazy. He quickly scanned the dark street, searching for someone who could help him, but there was no one in sight. It was too late and Britta's neighbors would probably already be fast asleep.

"Leave me alone!" His voice faltered. "I won't go back with you, okay? Why do you think I ran from you in the first place? I wasn't happy, Hunter!"

Hunter's face contorted into a smirk. "You think you're going to be happier with your new boyfriend? Is that it?"

Jake's gut clenched up into a knot. "What are you talking about?"

"Don't play stupid with me. I saw you both tonight."

Jake shuddered. "I don't know what you think you saw, but it doesn't matter. It doesn't concern you. We're over, Hunter."

Hunter scoffed and took a step forward, his towering figure looming over Jake. Another smirk settled itself on his face. "I forgive you," he said, in a deep, menacing tone. "We're all entitled to one mistake. Mine was not locking the door the day you ran out on me."

Jake shook his head a couple of times and opened his mouth in disbelief. "I'm not your property and I don't want you in my life anymore. Now, get out of my sight or—"

The world went white hot. The power of the slap thrust Jake's head to the side, and he instinctively took a sidestep to avoid falling to the sidewalk. A second later, his vision had returned but was filled with little green specks, more visible against the light of the street lamps.

Jake cupped his cheek. It was burning from the slap and he could feel the blood pulsing under the skin. As he looked up, he noticed Hunter was mouthing something with a furious expression, but couldn't really hear him. It was as though he was watching a movie in slow motion.

"Don't mess with me again! You hear me? Who do you think you are? I have told you, and I'm not going to repeat myself again. Get. Into. The CAR!"

Jake's hearing had returned. Hunter was screaming at him and shooting droplets of spittle everywhere. Jake couldn't ever remember seeing him this mad. For a moment, he feared Hunter would beat him until he complied. The next second, though, he felt overwhelmed by a rage he didn't know he had.

"If you touch me again, Hunter—"

This time, a punch hit him straight in his stomach. Jake felt the air leaving him and a sharp burn spreading through his gut. Hunter was bigger and stronger, and was making sure he understood who was in charge. The blow left Jake curled into an agonizing ball of pain on the sidewalk. From this perspective Hunter seemed even more dangerous.

"Step away from Jake or I'll unload this shotgun into your sorry little ass!"

Jake looked up. Britta was in her doorframe, pointing a shotgun at Hunter, her nightgown on and her hair caught up in a bun. Hunter stopped hovering over Jake and looked at her, panting.

"This is none of your business, lady. Go back inside."

"It's my business when you're beating a friend of mine. Now, get off of him or you'll be sorry." Britta pumped the shotgun. She had this menacing look on her face that Jake hadn't seen before.

Hunter raised his arms and scoffed. He looked at Jake, his eyes sparkling with rage. "It appears you've once again been saved by a gun. You better hope there's one nearby next time." He walked backwards, a defiant expression on his face, then got into his car and drove away.

Britta put the gun on the floor and ran to Jake. "Are you all right? Oh, my gosh. I assume that horrible guy is Hunter? You have the worst taste in men, Jake!"

Britta's barrage of words assaulted Jake's head like he had someone pounding a drum inside his skull. He winced when she tried to help him up. His face throbbed from the slap and a dull ache still radiated from his stomach and throughout his gut.

"Yeah, that's a mistake I'm still paying for dearly…" Jake whimpered.

"You should learn to defend yourself. The next time that jerk comes around, you could show him a thing or two."

Jake tried to laugh but a sharp pain made him pant instead. "Yeah, you're right. Like Krav Maga or something." Jake put his arm around Britta's neck and limped along the short path to her house.

"It doesn't have to be something out of special ops. As long as it keeps you safe." Britta looked at Jake who was wincing with each step he took. "We should go to the hospital."

For a second, Jake felt compelled to agree but then remembered he didn't have insurance and was out of a job. "I'm fine. I just need to lay a bit on the couch and maybe have some ice on my face."

They went into the house and Britta helped Jake to the couch. As he sat, Jake exhaled, relieved.

"Wait here for a second. I'll get some ice."

As Britta left, Jake realized what had happened. Suddenly, the world felt dangerous again, a cold and unrelenting place where it was eat or be eaten. He took a deep breath and tried to relax. He just had to be more careful next time and… Jake scoffed. And what? Punch Hunter? Run from him? Neither was a solution for his predicament and he didn't know exactly what to do. Maybe he should leave town and go somewhere else in the hopes Hunter would lose his track.

Britta returned a couple of minutes later with a bag full of ice and a kitchen cloth. "Here you go, honey," she said, wrapping the bag in the cloth.

The ice felt like heaven on his face, but a second later it was throbbing from the pain and the cold. He cringed and took the bag from his face, but without it the pain was even worse.

"Are you sure you don't want to go to the hospital?"

"I'm sure."

"You seem in a lot of pain."

"I'll be fine. Can we talk about something else? To take my mind off of this?"

"Sure, honey," she said, her hands on her lap.

Jake concentrated on the cold imparted by the ice for a moment, before saying: "How come you knew I needed help?"

"I was in the living room, reading my book when I heard a commotion. I went to the window and saw that awful man punching you. I had to do something."

Jake tried to smile, but couldn't. His face burned too much. "Well, I know I used to tease you about your liking guns, but I'm really glad you had that shotgun with you."

Britta slapped him gently on his arm. "See? This is a perfect example of what I used to say to you back in high school," she said, frowning.

"Yeah, well, I still think guns are mainly a menace."

Britta's brow furrowed. She chuckled. "Maybe we should change the subject."

"I think we should," he agreed, turning his head to her.

"How was it with Craig?"

Craig. He'd almost forgot about his night. "Wonderful, actually. Well, up until Hunter, that is."

"I still think you should go to the police. Especially after this. And Craig must be leaving in the next few days. You don't want to be looking over your shoulder when you could be enjoying the rest of your time with him."

Jake felt a sudden rush of adrenaline to his stomach. "What? Craig's leaving?"

"You know he's only here visiting his dad, right?"

"I had forgotten about that."

He sure had. And now that he'd remembered it, the possibility of Craig leaving was threatening to kill his mood much more than Hunter's appearance and assault.

CHAPTER 14

THE NEXT DAY, Jake was still a bit sore but at least his face wasn't a huge swollen lump. The only mark from his encounter with Hunter was a slight bruise on his jaw from the brutish slap. He sighed, relieved, looking into the mirror in the bathroom. The last thing he wanted to do was to worry his mother. It was chemo day and he'd promised to take her. He didn't want her worrying about any other stuff.

The night had been rough. He hadn't slept very well, turning and tossing on account of what Britta had said. He'd totally forgotten about Craig only being here to visit his father. He'd been so caught up with Hunter, his own father and trying to impress Craig that this had been dragged to somewhere deep inside his subconscious. And now he couldn't stop thinking about it. He felt like he'd wasted too much time and should have acted sooner on his newfound crush. Then again, he'd only realized it three days ago.

He left the room and went downstairs, dragging his feet. Not only was he sleepy but he felt anxious and discouraged by the fact that Craig could leave town at any minute. Was he a fling to him? What had he meant last night in the car, when he told him he'd get his chance at pleasing him? That implied that there was time, that he was planning to stay in town for a while, right?

"Hey, honey. What you doing up so early?" Britta was already in the kitchen, drinking her morning coffee and reading something on her tablet.

"Trouble sleeping," he said, approaching the counter.

"Is your face still hurting?"

"Not really…." He paused, embarrassed to admit his face didn't hurt as badly as his heart because he couldn't stop thinking about Craig. "Do you know when Craig's leaving?"

Britta put the tablet on the countertop, watching him with knowing eyes. "You're smitten. You're totally smitten with him," she said, giggling.

Jake blushed. He was going to deny it, but what was the point, anyway? "Is it that obvious?"

"Totally."

Jake sighed. He leaned forward, put his elbow on the countertop and his chin on his hand. "Maybe I'm a bad person. It's like you said. How the hell can I be head over heels for Craig when my mother is going through cancer? I should be worrying about her, not falling for him."

"I certainly didn't want you to think that, honey," Britta said, shaking her head. "Besides, yesterday I was a mess because of Eric."

"And how are you today? Do you know what you're gonna do?"

"No, but I won't hang around and mope about the jerk. I'll come up with a plan. Don't worry."

Jake smiled. "If that's the case, I'm just gonna pour myself a cup of coffee and go for a run. I'm really glad you think that way. Don't want to see you suffer over some idiot who can't even see the five-star gal he has home."

Britta blushed and her eyes welled. "You're damn right," she said, her voice quivering.

He got up and went to the coffee machine. "You think I could borrow your car for a couple of hours? I promised my mom I'd take her to her chemo appointment."

"Sure, honey."

***

The drive to the clinic was a short one but Jake constantly had to assure his mother that his bruise was nothing. He didn't want her to worry about Hunter so, instead of telling her the truth, he just said it was from his dad's slap.

"How are things, mom?" he asked, trying to change the subject.

She pressed her lips together and her gaze fell to some distant point down the road. "Your father still doesn't want to talk about you. I think he feels like he's lost his son." Her voice quivered.

A rush of blood warmed Jake's face. "Well, too bad. I'm done trying to please him so he can mourn my loss all he wants…" He stopped himself. It wouldn't do any good if he went on a rant about how awful a man he was. "But I meant with you, mom. How are things with you?"

"I'm fine."

"You don't look fine. You seem paler and those dark patches beneath your eyes are bigger."

"It's nothing, don't worry."

Jake parked the car right in front of the clinic. "You sure you're okay?"

"Yes, dear. The chemo has been making me a bit queasy the last couple of days. Nothing to worry about."

Jake got out of the car and went round to help his mother out, and suddenly it dawned on him how frail she was. For a split second he imagined the worst, a life where she would get sicker and he wouldn't be able to help her. His eyes welled up and he turned his head away. He didn't want her to see him crying.

His mother took the few steps into the clinic and he closed the car door, clearing the tears with the back of his hand. He took a couple of deep breaths and followed her in.

The building was what you'd expect from any other clinic: white, angular, slightly menacing considering the purpose of their visit. As soon as they went inside, Jake was assaulted by that peculiar smell that always lingered in such places, like disinfectant and something else he couldn't quite place. They went to the reception desk and it took only a couple of minutes for his mother to be shown the way to her treatment.

"Will you wait for me, dear? Should I call you when I'm ready?"

"I'll wait here, mom."

Jake had his book and was actually looking forward to reading it here. The thought that there were people in this world struggling with real problems made him put his own issues in perspective and reset his problem's gauge. After all, what was a jealous and crazy ex-boyfriend compared to cancer?

Jake kissed his mother on the cheek and went to sit in the waiting room. He grabbed his book and tried to immerse himself in it. He'd borrowed it from Britta before leaving the house. It was a gay romance, something he'd never expected to see in Britta's book stash. But, as she happily told him, she actually preferred those to straight romances. Those were far too syrupy for her.

The start felt a bit cheesy but Jake wasn't really looking for something that would teach him about quantum physics. He just wanted a light read that would help him forget about

Hunter. And, who knew? Maybe the book had some interesting sex ideas he could try with Craig. He blushed at the thought. *Stop with this nonsense, already. It's not like you're dating him.* And then his heart sank. He had to find out when Craig was leaving.

"Jake?"

He looked up. There was a guy staring at him, smiling. For a moment he thought he knew him but couldn't quite put a name to his face. And then, he recognized him.

"Michael? Oh, my God, it is you!" Jake got up, hugging him. Michael was one of the very few people he'd considered a friend back in high school. "What are you doing here?" His good humor vanished quickly when he realized where they were and what that probably meant. "Oh, I'm sorry. Stupid question to ask," he added, dropping his shoulders and feeling embarrassed.

"No, no. It's fine. I'm a volunteer here. Started a couple of years ago. Remember how I was always down, back in high school?"

"Yeah, I remember."

"As it turns out, I just had to give something back to the community. It's so good to help these people."

Jake's brain took note of his words. Maybe he just needed to focus on someone else instead of himself and his own fears would go away."

"Are you here with your mother?" Michael asked.

"Yeah, I brought her. How did you know?"

"I've seen her here a few times. Talk to her occasionally. But I haven't seen you in a long time. How are things?"

Jake didn't answer immediately. He was torn between telling him everything and not knowing what to say given where they were.

"Long story short, I moved back here after college but things aren't that great with my father."

"Yeah. I remember him being a...a difficult person."

"You can say that."

"Listen, I'm running late to work, but we should catch up one of these days. Maybe we could call Britta and gather the whole gang."

"I'm actually staying at her place for a while."

"You are?" He furrowed his brow, confusion plastered all over his face. "Okay. I'll call her and we'll think of something. Here's my number anyway. It was really nice to see you again."

And with that, Michael left. Jake looked at the piece of paper where he'd scribbled his phone number and remembered him back in high school as the kid always dressed in black, mourning for his life. As Jake sat back down, he observed the people around him. There were far greater problems in the world than his own insecurities and fear of living. Most of those people couldn't afford the luxury of wasting their lives being depressed about not having whatever it was they wanted.

I'm a really, really dumb ass. Why am I moping around just because Craig might leave? Do something about it, damn it. He decided in that moment that he'd start living his life to the fullest; beginning with Craig. And he'd start writing. Even if no one would want to read his stories.

Jake grabbed his phone.

Want to have dinner tonight?

As he pressed the send button, he felt good about this. There were worse things in life than Hunter. And he shouldn't be worried about how Craig felt about him. It was clear enough. The night before had been wonderful, especially the part where Craig confessed that he used to have a crush on him back in high school. Jake felt his dick tingling when he remembered Craig's lips around it. *Yeah. What am I afraid of anyway?*

CHAPTER 15

JAKE'S MOTHER WAS returning from her treatment when his phone buzzed. It was Craig.

I'd love to have dinner with you. I was actually thinking of inviting you but you beat me to it :)

Jake smiled and forced himself not to do a happy dance. That would be completely inappropriate considering where he was. He put the phone in his pocket and rushed to meet his mother.

"How're you feeling?"

She shook her head slightly and gave him her arm. Her lips were pressed together and the dark circles under her eyes were bigger.

"She's a bit tired and nauseated," said a nurse, behind them. "But she should be fine. She's a fighter, aren't you, Mrs. Taylor? Call me if you need something, okay?"

Jake's smile vanished and his heart sank. "Can I have your number? Just in case..." he asked the nurse.

The nurse gave him a card. "Maybe you could get her a bottle of sparkling water. Sometimes it helps to calm an upset stomach."

"I will. Thank you". The nurse left and Jake turned his attention to his mother again. "Do you want sparkling water?"

"No, thank you, dear. I'm fine. I just want to go home," she said, almost in a whisper.

The short walk to the car was made slowly, his mother leaning on him, lighter than ever. He helped her sit in her seat and closed the door, taking a deep breath. She'd be fine. She had to be.

As he walked around to the driver's side, his eyes were drawn to a car parked on the other side of the road. It was a black sedan but it looked familiar. So familiar, in fact, that he looked more closely. He saw Hunter, watching him through an open window, chewing gum. His heart raced and he hurried to his car.

"Is something wrong?" his mother asked feebly as he sat behind the wheel.

Jake fumbled to put the keys in the ignition. "No, mom. Everything's fine. Try to rest."

He started the car and drove away as fast as he could, but, at the same time, trying not to startle his mother. The urge to step on the gas pedal was big, but he inhaled deeply three times to calm himself down.

Jake looked in the rear-view mirror and saw Hunter doing a U-turn and following them. He didn't seem in a hurry, just staying close enough not to lose sight of them. *What the hell is that jerk doing?* Fortunately, his mother was blissfully unaware of what was going on. She seemed to have dozed off and he was thankful for that.

He reached a red light and stopped. His heart pounded like a wild animal trying to break free from its cage. The lane next to him was empty. He was afraid Hunter would pull up alongside, and so he locked the doors. Jake looked in the mirror again and saw his car approaching. Hunter stopped behind them, chewing gum with his mouth open, his gaze on Jake's rear-view mirror. His look seemed menacing and his face showed a smirk. Why wasn't he stopping by his side?

Hunter honked the horn and Jake jumped. Through the mirror, he saw him looking up and pointing to somewhere in front and above them. He seemed amused. Jake's gaze moved from the mirror to the road and he noticed the light had turned green. He drove off, fuming.

When he parked at his parents' house, Hunter was still on his tail. He'd parked down the street but Jake could see him, watching him and his mother with preying eyes. He didn't know what was on his mind, but he didn't like it.

Jake helped his mother out of the car and into the house. He insisted on staying a bit longer but she wouldn't have it. She said she'd be fine and that was that. Besides, his father could arrive any minute and she wanted to avoid a fight. So did Jake, not because of him but for her sake. He left, although he didn't want to.

Hunter was still parked down the road. Jake got in the car, drove away and called Britta.

"Britta? Hi, it's me. Are you home?... Good. Could you wait for me by the door with your shotgun?... No, no, everything's fine but Hunter's been following me since I left the clinic with my mother... Yes, he followed us to her house... No, don't call the police... No, Britta. I don't want the police involved. Could you just wait for me with...with the gun, yes. I'm coming over now. See you in a bit." He hung up and looked back. Hunter was still behind him.

The drive to Britta's home was a short one. Jake kept looking in the mirror, hoping that maybe Hunter would go away, but he didn't. He parked the car in front of the house, honking to let Britta know he had arrived but it wasn't really necessary. Britta was already at the door, waiting for him. Jake got out of the car and hurried to the house, looking over his shoulder. Britta walked a bit further down the driveway and cocked the gun. They both saw Hunter slowing down as he drove by, a smirk on his face, and then he sped up again.

"That's right, you jerk. You better leave," she shouted as Hunter drove away. She turned to Jake, pointing at Hunter's car. "That guy's nuts. I really think we should go to the police."

He shook his head. "I don't think that's necessary."

"Why not? For all we know, he's dangerous. I think it's best—"

"I said no, Britta," he said, louder than he'd intended. Britta watched him, eyes wide, brows furrowing a bit. "I'm sorry. I didn't mean to speak to you like that."

She sighed. "Apology accepted. But can you at least tell me why not?"

Jake's gaze drifted from her to the ground. When he looked up again, there was a glaze covering his eyes. He entered the house. Britta hurried to the door and followed him in.

"I just don't want to be mocked again," he finally said when Britta closed the door behind her.

"What are you talking about?"

Jake sighed as he sat on the couch. "I went to the police a couple of months ago, and told them I was afraid of Hunter, that he was aggressive." Jake paused and then scoffed. "The guy I spoke to could barely disguise his nausea every time he looked at me and things only got worse from there on in. He took me to this colleague of his who dealt with domestic abuse…" Jake scoffed again. "He laughed at me when he heard my story, so I left."

Britta listened in silence, open-mouthed. Her pale complexion had got redder as she'd heard his story. "What the hell is wrong with people?" she almost shouted. She was, by now, pacing the room.

"I don't want to go through that again. I have you and Craig. I'm not alone anymore, and I don't want to go to the police, okay?"

"You should've done something about those idiot cops. It's not right."

"I just wanted to get out of there."

Britta sighed and sat down by Jake's side. "You do realize that not everyone is like those jerks, right? There are still good people on this planet."

"I know," he said, smiling. "I just don't want to deal with this right now." There it was. He was again trying to run from something. Last time he'd done that, it had gone after him. And by "it", he meant Hunter. "Right now I want to focus on my dinner with Craig tonight."

"You two are going out, with that lunatic out there looking for you?"

"I refuse to give in to fear, Britta. I intend to make the most of the time Craig's here. And don't worry: I'll be extra careful."

"And when Craig leaves?"

Jake shrugged. That was the million dollar question. "I really don't know."

CHAPTER 16

JAKE SPENT THE rest of his afternoon thinking of what he'd do when Craig left. He kept jumping from scenario to scenario, a circular rut that kept bringing him to the same conclusion. He could go with Craig to San Francisco and try get a job there, but the city was crazy expensive and he was sure he wouldn't be able to afford a bedroom, let alone an apartment. It was crazy to think of it anyway: he'd only gone out with Craig the once and was already planning a whole life with him. What if Craig didn't like him enough for that? What if this was just a fling, something to ease the loneliness of a small town like theirs? Instead of wondering, he should just ask him and be done with it. What had he to lose, anyway? A week ago, Craig wasn't even part of his life so he shouldn't be afraid of knowing what was going to happen with them.

Oh, my god. You are going to scare him away with your questions and your ideas. He'll think you're nuts! Let it go, already!

And it would start all over again: go to San Francisco, get a job, find a place, realize it was a silly idea even to talk to Craig about their "relationship" that, in fact, was just one date at a bar.

So it was a relief when Jake saw it was time to leave for Craig's house.

"I'm off to dinner. See you later," he said, knocking at Britta's bedroom door.

She opened the door a second later, when Jake was already on the stairs. "Is he picking you up here?"

Jake stopped and looked over his shoulder. "No. Actually, I'm walking to his house. He wanted to leave everything prepared for the evening, in case his father needed something. Why?"

"Because of that creep. For all we know he could be down the road waiting for you."

Jake had forgotten about him. "I'll be careful, I promise. Besides, it's a short walk to his dad's. I'll be fine, don't worry."

"Don't be silly. I'll give you a lift. I won't let you out of that door all alone, and that's the end of it."

***

The drive to Craig's house was uneventful. Hunter was nowhere to be seen and that was even more unnerving than knowing he was parked somewhere down the street.

Britta left Jake in Craig's street and drove away, bidding him a wonderful evening. He then stood in front of Craig's door for a minute, breathing deeply. He felt nervous but didn't know quite why. Maybe it was because he was going to meet Craig's dad and that made this an almost formal affair; like he was being introduced to his family or something. Totally ridiculous, of course.

He rang the bell and waited. The street was chilly and quiet, except for the whistling trees, dancing from the occasional gust of wind. Jake pulled his coat closer as a shiver ran through him. He heard footsteps and then the door opened.

"You're here," Craig said, an expansive smile dancing across his face. "Come in. It's freezing out there."

Jake smiled back, feeling Craig's grin embracing him and displacing the cold of the night.

"So, this is the young man who's been making my son so happy lately," Craig's dad said when Jake entered the house. His face turned beet red but he wasn't the only one.

"Dad, don't say that. He's right here!"

"Why not if it's true?" the old man asked while getting up from his armchair to meet Jake.

"Because you don't know what you're talking about and you're embarrassing me." Craig's reprimand was only half-hearted, but he was genuinely embarrassed. Jake could see it in his face.

"It's very nice to meet you, Mr. Mathews," Jake said, shaking his hand.

"And you too, young man." Mr. Mathews slightly tilted his head while his eyes examined Jake. "You're bruised. Are you okay?"

Craig turned to Jake. "What happened?" he asked, approaching Jake's face, having not seen the light bruise on his face because it had been dark outside.

"It's nothing. I just banged my face this morning when I was still half asleep." He didn't want to lie, but it was only a white lie after all. And Mr. Mathews didn't have to know about his story with Hunter.

"Well, in that case you take good care of my Craig. I'm going upstairs to my bedroom. Have a good night." As he left, he pointed his finger at Craig. "Don't mess this up, okay? I have a good feeling about this one."

Mr. Mathews' words created a bubble of nervous laughter in Jake's chest that wanted to erupt in a giggle. He already liked the old man and wished his own dad could be a little more like him.

The thought burst his bubble. He sighed and blocked it. There was no need to dwell on things that were out of his control and ruin the night.

"Good night, dad. If you need something, just call me, okay?"

Mr. Mathews waved his hand while he walked up the stairs, his pace slow, without looking back. They both observed him in silence as he disappeared into the upstairs corridor. Jake heard the sound of a door closing. Craig turned around and approached Jake. His gaze swept him for a second and then he kissed him, holding his head in his hands, a soft kiss that left Jake shaking and his head spinning.

"I'm sorry about that," Craig said, after taking his lips away from Jake's. "He just can't wait for me to get a partner and never loses an opportunity to encourage me. I think he's feeling down because of my mother and doesn't want me to be alone like him."

Jake's head was still spinning. "It's so nice of him to support you. Really sweet." Jake took off his coat. It was really warm inside. Or maybe it was the kiss. "He must miss your mother very much."

"He does. I don't know what else to do. The neighbors have been very supportive but he seems to have given up." Craig paused for a second. "I'm sorry. I guess meeting here wasn't the best idea."

Jake smiled. He went to an armchair and put his coat down. "Don't be silly. It's nice to see how your father cares about you."

Craig's eyes zoomed in on Jake's jaw. "What happened to you, anyway?" he asked, drawing near to Jake and gently touching his face. "Did your father hit you again?"

"No. I haven't seen him since the other day." He didn't know if he should tell Craig about Hunter or not. "This was Hunter."

"What? What happened? Are you all right?" Craig, said, holding Jake's head and examining him, looking for more bruises. A second later, though, he let him go. He seemed embarrassed by his own reaction.

"I'm fine. He was waiting for me yesterday and appeared out of nowhere after you left."

"Why didn't you tell me?"

"It was late and Britta was there. She scared him away with her shotgun."

Craig's brows furrowed a bit. "She did?"

"Yeah. She's a real bad-ass."

Craig sighed. "You should've called me."

"Why? There was nothing you could do."

Craig drew nearer. "I could've been there for you."

Jake smiled. "I'll call you next time."

"Next time? I really hope there isn't going to be a 'next time'."

Jake was again reminded of the fact that Craig would be leaving soon. His gaze fell on Craig's eyes. He was going to say something, ask him about it, but he thought otherwise. What was the point? If he was going to leave, Jake might as well enjoy him while he was in town, instead of ruining everything.

You were supposed to be the captain of your destiny, remember? What're you afraid of?

Indeed. What was he afraid of? Craig no longer liking him as soon as he asked him when was he leaving? No, that wasn't it. Maybe deep down he believed Craig was just having a good time and it was all a fling. Maybe he was really afraid of discovering his feeling for Craig was much more powerful than he thought. Maybe he loved Craig.

What! Love? Don't be ridiculous. You don't love him. Sure, you're constantly thinking about him, and he melts your insides, but that's because you feel vulnerable. That's all.

"Is everything okay? You seem distant."

Jake's eyes focused on him. "No, no, I'm fine. Really."

"You know what you could do? You could take a self-defense class," Craig said with a half-smile.

"Funny you should mention that. Britta said the same thing."

"Really? Because I was going to say I could teach you if you want."

Jake felt his heartbeat speeding up. "Really? And what do you know about self-defense?"

Craig smiled. "I've been taking taekwondo for several years, now."

"Oh, I see. So you must be a real menace," Jake said, chuckling.

Craig got even nearer, mere inches from his face. Jake could see his pores, the subtle changes in color in his eyes, feel his body heat.

"I think I am," Craig said. He leaned in and kissed Jake softly, grabbing him by his waist. Jake's worries were cast aside. He couldn't think of them, didn't care. All he cared about were those soft lips pressed against his own, converting his legs into a mass of jelly incapable of supporting him.

Craig leaned back, his gaze sweeping Jake, a big smile expanding across his face. "Shall we go?"

Jake's heartbeat still pounded in his head. He had completely forgotten about dinner and would rather have stayed here, nestled in his big, strong arms. "Do we have to?"

"Well, I'm starving. And my dad's upstairs…"

"What? A bit cocky, no?" Jake said, pushing him back with one finger pressed to his left pec.

Craig laughed, throwing his head back. He was so wonderful and genuine.

"I'm not cocky. I wasn't implying *that*. I was trying to say that we can't order in because my dad will be asleep soon and I don't want to wake him up." His brows were raised in an ascending arc, trying to make his expression innocent. Jake's insides melted into a puddle of wax.

"You're so cute," he said, brushing the back of his hand on Craig's cheek. "I don't know how it is that you're single, but I'm glad you are."

Craig didn't answer but kissed him instead.

CHAPTER 17

CRAIG SUGGESTED THEY go for a ride after dinner and they ended up going down to the old lookout point where all the teenagers used to hook up. After teasing him as to why he wanted to go somewhere everyone knew was a favorite make out spot for teens, Jake ended up saying it was a good idea. After all, it was halfway up to the woods and had a beautiful view over the town.

All this talking over dinner about teens, hook ups and life made Jake realize he was falling hard for Craig. Suddenly he was seeing him in a different light, like he'd opened his eyes and now saw the most beautiful man in front of him. Craig was funny, charming, cute, intelligent... There were so many good things about him that Jake didn't really know which one he liked the most. His mood swung wildly between feeling like he could swoon at any moment and a melancholy caused by the certainty that moments like these were ephemeral and would soon disappear when Craig left town. He'd spent his life trying to understand what people meant by heartache, and now he knew. He felt a compression in his chest, like someone had a hand inside him, holding his heart, squeezing it tight. It was hard to breathe.

Craig stopped the car and they got out. The view was amazing but the air was chilly. Jake had forgotten how small the town seemed from up here and how its twinkling lights reminded him of the stars above.

A minute later, he was shivering.

"This is really breathtaking but I think I'm gonna go back to the car," he said.

"Come here," Craig said, grabbing his arm. He hugged Jake and put his coat around him. Jake could hear Craig's heartbeat, feel his body heat and smell his manly aroma. His heart squeezed a little bit more and he sighed, allowing himself to melt in the warm embrace. He felt a knot closing his throat but tried to ignore it. He was scared of the intensity of his own feelings. It was all becoming a bit too much to bear, no matter how much he fooled himself. He wasn't in control of his life, his heart was. And it kept telling him he was in love with Craig.

Jake felt a pressure inside of him building up. He stopped breathing, trying to control it, willing it to go away. He didn't want to cry. He wouldn't. He closed his eyes with all his might and ignored the pressure that continued to rise. *Don't cry. Don't cry!* Something snapped and a great big sob escaped him. Jake shuddered and held tighter to Craig.

"What's wrong?" Craig asked, looking down. Jake had buried his face deeper into Craig's chest.

Jake let a couple of sobs out before whispering: "Everything... You're leaving and I'm not gonna see you again..."

"Whoa. Who said I was leaving?" Craig said, holding Jake by his shoulders.

Jake wiped the tears from his face with the back of his hand. "You did, remember? You said you were only here visiting your dad."

"That's right, but you said it like I was leaving you. I'm not leaving you."

Jake shuddered and sniffed. "You're not?"

Craig hugged him again, tighter this time. "I've not stopped thinking about you ever since I saw you on Britta's doorstep. I've been torn between calming myself and letting the feelings grow but I can't help it. I want you, Jake. More now, even."

Jake's tears dried as soon as Craig had said he couldn't stop thinking about him, vaporized by the fire in his words. He smiled and looked up. Craig's gaze bathed him and freed him of his angst. Craig leaned down and kissed him, sending pleasure ripples throughout his body. His fears were swept away, washed by a certainty that there was something between them, that Craig didn't consider this only a fling.

Jake's dick twitched against Craig's crotch.

"Well, hello there," Craig said, grinning, still pressing his lips against Jake's. Jake chuckled, overflowing with happiness, while Craig grabbed his arm and dragged him into the car.

"I think this is my first time in the back of a car," Jake said as Craig pinned him against the seat. He felt a giggle inside trying to escape, but managed to control it. Only his grin showed how nervous he was.

"I promise I'll take good care of you," Craig said, a half-smile dancing on his face. He kissed him, a soft, gentle kiss that brushed his lips and made Jake's insides melt. The brush grew stronger and Craig held Jake's face in his hands, his mouth pressing firmer against Jake's, exploring and teasing. Craig ran one hand down his neck and pulled his jacket back. He parted from Jake's lips for a second, took off his own coat and put them both in the front seat.

"It's getting crowded in here," he said, leaning towards Jake again and kissing him, pinning him against the seat. Craig unbuttoned Jake's shirt and explored his chest with one hand, sliding it down towards his crotch. He cupped and then squeezed Jake's hard cock, whose shape was visible under his jeans. His hand backed up again to his neck and lingered there.

Jake was invaded by a heat, radiating from everywhere, concentrating itself wherever Craig's hand landed.

Jake kissed Craig back while pulling his shirt out of his pants. He undid its buttons and ran his hands over Craig's torso, properly touching him for the first time, exploring his shape, feeling him. He was all man, his frame strong as a brick wall. Jake's fingers explored his muscles and body hair, sprinkled on his pecs and abs, disappearing into his crotch. Jake's dick jumped when he ran his hand into Craig's jeans and felt his trimmed bush and then his cock. It was slippery with precum. Jake's heart thumped inside his ribcage and he felt a heatwave spreading throughout himself, concentrating itself on his ears and dick. Jake tried to grab it but Craig's jeans were too tight.

"My turn," Jake said feverishly, pushing Craig back. He unzipped Craig's jeans and pulled them down. Jake gasped when he saw his massive dick pulsing, freed from the confines of his boxer briefs. He took it in his mouth and ran his tongue over and around its head, feeling the salty taste of his precum.

"You taste so good," he said, coming up for a moment before taking his dick again. He bobbed his head a couple of times, going deeper each time, sensing it approaching his throat. Craig moaned, his hands desperately searching for something to hold on to, his chest rising and falling rapidly. Jake went deeper still, Craig's cock filling him.

Jake came up to breathe and his gaze traveled to Craig's eyes. He saw lust in them. *This is really happening.* He leaned forward and kissed Craig, the flavor of his cock still in his mouth. Craig's dick was now rubbing just above Jake's crotch, wet from saliva and precum. Jake moved his hips, rubbing himself against Craig's cock, pressing on the stiff shaft, feeling it expand with each heartbeat.

"I wanna fuck you," Craig whispered in between ragged breaths.

"You do?" Jake whispered, teasing him.

Craig didn't answer back. He broke away from Jake's kiss and pushed him into the seat, laying him down, pinning his hands above his head. "I do," he said. He kissed Jake's neck and travelled to his torso, nibbling on his nipples. Craig unzipped Jake's pants, pulling them and his boxer shorts down in one swift move. He spit on his index and middle fingers and rubbed them on Jake's asshole, massaging and teasing him, threatening to fuck him but never quite entering. Jake gasped in surprise and blood rushed to his ass. Craig took his fingers out and again spat on his hand. This time, though, it was to lube his massive cock. He pulled Jake's legs up, over his own shoulders, and guided his dick to Jake's hole.

Jake could feel Craig's bulging head pressing against his ass, forcing itself in before quickly retreating. His heartbeat was now down there, pulsing in his anus as he felt Craig's massive head pushing for a moment and then again backing up. He thought he wouldn't be able to take such a massive cock but the fear lasted only a fleeting moment. Craig thrust his cock inside, a swift movement that opened him up. Jake gasped but Craig was already inside, a firehose that filled him completely.

"Are you alright?" Craig whispered.

"Fuck me!" Jake said, grabbing his arms.

Craig thrust again, and again, each thrust pressing his cock further up until it reached Jake's prostate. Jake's eyes lit up when he felt it, a mix of sensations rushing inside him, the world around extinguished by a shower of endorphins shooting from his brain. Craig thrust a few more times and Jake felt like he was cumming from the inside, like Craig was jerking him off without touching his dick.

"I'm... coming!" Jake managed to say, as he felt his juices leaking out of his dick. He grabbed himself, wanting to extend the feeling. As soon as his fingers wrapped around his cock, though, he fire-hosed his load all over himself, a white, thick heat that seemed as though it would never end. Craig grunted at the same time and Jake felt his dick expand, warm cum gushing inside him.

Craig fell on top of Jake and they lay there, motionless, spent, panting, trying to catch their breaths as together they fell into an oblivion of pure bliss.

CHAPTER 18

A SHIVER RAN down Jake's spine, pulling him from the dream state in which his mind had floated. He opened his eyes and saw Craig right next to him, part of his body on top of him still, the rest lying on the backseat. They must've fallen asleep. Jake felt the cold air on his exposed skin. He tried to move but couldn't. Craig was too heavy, even with only part of his body on top of him.

Jake grinned when he realized where he was and what had just happened. A bubble of happiness expanded inside his chest and took him over. He ran his free hand over Craig's torso, feeling his warmth, his rock-solid frame.

"Hmm, that feels good," Craig moaned in a sleepy voice.

"I think we fell asleep."

"I think you're right."

Craig sat up on the backseat and Jake did the same. Their clothes were piled up on the car's floor, a messy proof of their recent passion.

"Oh, shit. It's late," Craig said, looking at his watch. "We should get back. Do you mind? I'm worried my father might wake up and need something."

Jake felt his bubble expand a bit more. "You are so wonderful," he said, a wide grin set on his face.

Craig smiled back and kissed him, a long, soft kiss that made Jake's bones melt into jelly.

They dressed quickly and Craig started the car. As they drove back to town, Jake glanced at the mountains, thinking how beautiful the town was from afar. Sadly, the same couldn't be said of its people. The engine's noise lulled him almost into a trance. He felt relaxed, happy and safe. Craig's fingers were intertwined with his, his warm hand reassuring him that he hadn't hallucinated any of it. Craig was really here and he had really just experienced the most amazing sex ever. It had almost felt like making love, except it was too soon and too complicated to be in love with Craig. *Just enjoy what you have and don't think of anything else. Don't ruin the moment.*

"I want to see you again tomorrow," Craig said, after stopping the car in front of Britta's house. His face glowed with caring and Jake wanted to lose himself in his beautiful brown-green eyes again.

Jake leaned over and kissed him, feeling his sweet, full lips, parting them with his tongue and exploring his mouth. "That would make me very happy."

After entering Britta's house and closing the front door, Jake leaned his back on it and looked up. He was so happy. He couldn't remember ever being so happy.

"I take it the night went well judging from that grin on your face," Britta said, giggling. She was sitting on the couch, her laptop in front of her. Jake almost jumped, so lost was he in his own thoughts.

"It was wonderful," he said, unable to extinguish his smile. He sat by her side. "I'm so happy. I never knew it was possible to be this happy," he said while taking off his coat.

Britta chuckled again. "I'll say. I think I'm catching a bit of your happiness. Look at me, giggling like an idiot."

Jake laughed.

"And what are you doing here, sitting almost in the dark?"

"Applying for a job. I want to go back to college as soon as possible and for that I need money. I'm trying not to use the money my mother left me."

Jake's smile vanished and he pursed his lips. He felt guilty for being so happy. "Have you talked to Eric? How are things?"

"I don't know. I guess he's still 'working'. But you know what? I really don't care. I'm tired of sitting here trying to figure out what he's doing, wondering if he's sleeping with another woman or not. It's like you wake up one day and you suddenly realize you've become an awful, insecure person whose happiness depends on someone that doesn't care about you."

"Don't say that. You're not an awful person. If anything, it's him who's treating you like this."

"No, no. It's a good thing. I finally saw what I've become and what I have to do to get out of this rut I'm in."

"Okay, but please don't say you're awful. You're not—"

Jake was interrupted by the sound of a cell phone ringing. He waited for Britta to answer it.

"You're not gonna get that?" he asked.

"What? I thought it was your phone. It's coming from you."

Jake noticed the sound *was* coming from his coat. "No… I… This isn't mine." He felt his jacket, trying to find the origin of the sound. He finally found a phone in its left pocket. He picked it up. The screen read "Dad's home". "I think this is Craig's."

"Well, answer it."

"Hello? Craig… Yeah, I have it… It was in my coat pocket… Yeah, I think you put it here by mistake while…"

Jake's face turned red as his eyes travelled to Britta. "Sure, no problem. Bye."

"Well?" Britta asked with a huge grin on her face.

"I must have picked up Craig's phone when we were coming back to town. It's late and he doesn't want to leave the house again. He's coming by tomorrow."

Britta chuckled. "I'm sorry, but it's hard not to laugh when your face looks like that," she said, pointing at him.

"What?"

"It's just that you seem embarrassed and happy, all at the same time. It's weird!"

"I am! This night was so wonderful, I—"

The phone buzzed again and Jake's gaze fell to its screen. His eyes went dark and his grin vanished.

"What's wrong, honey? Is everything okay?" Britta said, putting her laptop aside.

Jake didn't answer. He was mute, weeping in silence, his body shaken by an occasional tremor.

"Honey, what is it? You're making me nervous," Britta said, gently stroking his shoulder a couple more times. Jake looked up, consumed by grief, sobbing in silence while fat tears ran down his face. Britta took the phone from him and read the text on the screen.

"I miss you and your cock. Come back soon!"

Britta gasped, lifting her gaze to Jake. "No, no, honey. It can't be. Craig wouldn't do this to you. It must be some kind of mistake"

"It's fine," Jake said in a whisper, running his hand beneath his nose. "Really. We're all adults, right? It was stupid of me to assume that a guy like him would be alone…" Jake's voice broke as he finished the sentence.

"Being an adult has nothing to do with this. Craig wouldn't deceive you. He's not like that."

Jake opened his mouth but said nothing. Instead, a big, loud sob escaped as his shoulders dropped, heavy with the weight of the world. How could he be so stupid? Why did he think a guy as handsome as Craig would want anything with him, apart from a one night fuck? Of course he had someone back in San Francisco. Of course that someone was waiting for him.

He couldn't fathom how Craig could be this charming and have a fuck on the side at the same time. How could he do this to that other guy? Did they have an arrangement? Arrangement or not, Jake felt dirty, like he was being used to satisfy Craig's urges. At least with Hunter he knew what to expect. There was no deceit there. But Craig… He thought Craig was different, a good guy, someone who cared enough about his father to be with him for a week to make sure he didn't feel lonely; to make sure he was starting to get over his wife's death. This… This was low. This was something that even Hunter wouldn't do. This was trying to pass for a good guy when in reality he was no such thing.

Britta put the phone down and hugged Jake. He burrowed his face in her shoulder and his silent sobbing broke into a wailing that even he hadn't expected. As Jake listened to his own cries, a little voice inside his head kept telling him to shut up because he was embarrassing himself. What he and Craig had didn't warrant this kind of pain, did it? But he didn't care for the voice or for what he had had with Craig. He was crying for himself and the lack of love in his life, for having spent so much time in the grip of a sociopath who thought he was his property, for his father and the hate he felt for his own son. Jake let himself dwell on the feeling that maybe he didn't deserve to be happy. Maybe the kind of intimacy he longed for was just something out of his reach.

"It's okay, honey. I'm here for you." Britta cradled him for a bit, but was interrupted by the doorbell. She looked at the door and again at Jake. "Let me just check on that. It might be important." Britta nudged Jake's head to the couch and got up, dashing to the door. As she opened it, her mouth fell.

"Craig... What are you doing here?"

"Hi. I know it's late but I just came to pick up my phone... And also to see Jake," he said, approaching her with a big grin. Britta stepped outside and closed the door behind her.

"I'm sorry but I don't think it's a good idea for you to come in. Please, don't hate me."

Craig furrowed his brow. "Sure.... Is everything okay?" he asked, tilting his head.

Britta hesitated. "I really don't want to be caught in the middle of this because I love you two... But you know what? What you did to Jake was really shitty, Craig. He's a nice kid and he didn't deserve this."

Craig jerked his head back. "What are you talking about?" he asked, wide-eyed.

Britta's face turned red. Maybe the situation was striking a chord with her but suddenly she felt angry. "I thought you were different, but apparently you're just as unable to keep it in your pants as the next guy. I'll get your phone. You wait here."

"Britta, wait. What are you talking about? I didn't do anything to Jake that he didn't want."

Britta said nothing and went inside, closing the door behind her. She grabbed the phone from the couch.

"Who was that?" Jake asked, squinting at Britta and wiping away tears with his hand. He looked all puffy and could barely open his eyes.

"It's no one. You stay here. I'll be right back—"

The door opened and Craig came inside. Jake looked up then jumped from the couch, his eyes darting between Craig and Britta.

"I'm sorry, but I don't understand what's—Jake, what happened?" he asked when he saw Jake's puffy eyes.

Jake opened his mouth but couldn't speak. He was now mute. Instead, big fat tears rolled down his face. Craig walked towards him but Jake ran up the stairs.

"Jake! Jake!" he called. He moved to follow but Britta stood in front of him. "What the hell is going on?" he said, locking eyes with her.

Britta's face was still red. Instead of speaking, she gave him his cell phone. Craig grabbed it and looked at the screen. Then he went pale.

"Oh, god…" he said. His gaze returned to Britta. "This doesn't mean what you think."

Britta looked at Craig askance, her lips pursed and a frown wrinkling her forehead. "You better have a damn good explanation for this."

CHAPTER 19

JAKE RAN TO the guest room and closed the door, soon pacing back and forth, the world blurred by tears. He was a stupid, stupid man for letting himself believe that someone like Craig could be interested in more than having sex with him. And why the hell was he assuming so much anyway? Why was he already picturing them as a couple, living together in a house surrounded by trees, a dog in the backyard? He shouldn't have let that feeling grow inside him. He should've squashed it as soon as he realized what was happening because he was doing it again, constructing a whole happy life with someone just because they had been nice to him. This lack of self-respect, this idea that happiness somehow depended on someone giving him affection had to stop. Where had it led him? Nowhere. No, not nowhere; somewhere chock full of deceit and pain. He had gone from a sociopath to a guy with two faces, someone else's leftovers.

"I miss your cock! Come back soon!"

His mind went into overdrive, imagining some cute guy waiting for Craig to return from his trip. The words were burned into his brain, a mental image he was desperately trying to erase but couldn't. Jake grimaced as he remembered them once again and felt his sorrow bloom into anger not only for having believed that Craig was a special guy but also at himself, for needing someone else in order to be happy; that need that had driven him to Hunter, that had blinded him to his true character, was once again failing him.

Jake shook his head. No, he couldn't believe Craig was a fake. How could he be? He recalled his brown-green eyes, the warmth that emanated from him, the way he spoke with him… He'd just had the most amazing sex of his life. It had seemed so real the way Craig had looked at him, saying he wasn't planning to abandon him. And now all of that was over, not even an hour later?

He stopped in his tracks, his gaze lost to the view through the window. "How could he have lied to me like that?" he said to no one.

His chest rose and fell rapidly. It was getting increasingly difficult to breathe, as if the bedroom's air was thickening, transforming into some kind of molasses that oozed around him. He felt a heat inside his stomach, radiating out to his face and burning his ears. He couldn't breathe. He needed to leave the house, to be surrounded by the cool, fresh breeze of the night. But Craig was downstairs.

Jake stopped pacing and his gaze swept the room, trying to think of a way to escape while avoiding Craig. The window! Was the drop too high? Jake strode to the window and opened it. He looked outside. Beneath it was the little shed Britta used to store her gardening tools. *The shed!* It was doable. Its roof was halfway to the ground and so he wouldn't have to jump more than ten feet and risk breaking an ankle.

He couldn't think of nothing but leaving the house. Jake couldn't stand being another minute here. Craig could come through his bedroom door at any time and he didn't know what he'd do if that happened. He only knew he wouldn't be able to bear it.

Jake looked over his shoulder at the room one last time. What was he doing? He didn't know and he didn't care.

He placed one leg over the windowsill, grabbed the frame and brought the other over, finally sitting on the sill. He turned himself around and onto his stomach, facing back into the room, his feet dangling beneath him, then grabbed the sill firmly with both hands. He lowered himself slowly, his feet scrabbling down the wall, acting as brakes, while he clung dearly to the windowsill. Once suspended at arm's length, he let himself go. The fall lasted hardly a second before he landed softly on the shed's roof.

I did it! His heart was racing, thumping in his ears. After a moment's hesitation, he sat at the edge of the roof, turned onto his knees and again lowered himself, falling to the ground when his hands slipped from the poor purchase of the shed's roofing felt. His legs faltered and he fell to his knees, but the grass was soft and cushioned his landing. Jake sprang to his feet and looked around before running towards the street.

Free, at last! The air felt so much cleaner and fresher! He could breathe again. Jake took a deep breath and gasped as he felt the chilly air stab at his lungs. He now realized he had left his coat behind and wasn't clothed enough to face the cold night. *Fuck!* He hadn't thought things through.

Jake looked around at the empty street. Where could he go? His parent's house was out of the question, of course, but he didn't know anybody else. The only option was the town's hotel. Maybe he could spend the night there and think about things in the morning. He'd always thought it was stupid having a hotel in a small town like this, but now he was thankful for it.

He hurried along the street as if being chased. The hotel was maybe a twenty minute walk and he needed to get there as soon as possible. Jake was already shivering but hoped the brisk pace would be enough to keep him warm.

A car passed by but then swerved across his path, coming to a halt right in front of him. Jake's heart almost broke free of his ribcage. *What kind of jerk does this?*

"Are you crazy? You almost ran me over, you idiot!" he shouted, gesturing angrily at the car with his closed fists. The door opened and a man stepped out. Jake immediately regretted what he'd said. The last thing he needed was an angry driver punching him. Then he saw who it was and his heart skipped a beat.

"Get into the car," Hunter said, pointing a gun at Jake and closing in on him. Jake stared at the barrel of the gun, not able to believe it. "I told you you'd better have a gun next time I saw you. Now, get in the car." Hunter's gun was now an inch away from Jake's chest.

Jake was in shock. He couldn't speak; he could only hear the noise of his heartbeat inside his chest, his blood roaring through his ears. Jake's mind was racing to find an escape, something that would help him flee this insane man. His eyes darted around madly, but there was no one to help him. He was trapped in a nightmare and somehow saw himself from a distance, like the whole ordeal was happening to someone else. Hunter pressed the gun against Jake's chest and he realized he'd no other choice. He had to do as he was told.

He walked towards the car, still not believing what was happening. Was this the end of it all? In a way, he almost deserved it. It served him right for being so naïve and weak. As he got into the car, Jake wondered if he would ever see his mother, Britta or Craig again.

CHAPTER 20

JAKE WAS AGAIN inside a moving car and again its engine was lulling him into a trance, but this time he wasn't thinking of Craig or the happiness that had embraced him just a few hours ago. Now he was just scared to death.

Hunter drove in silence and Jake considered his options. He could jump out of the car, but that would probably hurt him badly and he couldn't risk breaking a leg. And even if he somehow managed to land safely on the road and run for it, Hunter had a gun and Jake was pretty sure he couldn't sprint fast enough to dodge its bullets.

Jake stole a peek at Hunter. Who was this man? He knew he had a bad temper and was jealous, but this? This was a whole new level of craziness. He'd never pegged him as a murderer or a kidnapper. But here they were, driving at night along a now deserted road, a gun on Hunter's lap. The thought of trying to grab the gun from him crossed his mind, but he was sure he wasn't fast enough. But it sure was tempting. Hunter was focused on his driving and it was just a question of reaching for it. He looked again, this time turning his head a bit more, trying to see exactly where the gun was. On the other hand, he'd never fired a gun and didn't have a clue as to where to begin. He knew there was a trigger and he'd seen, in the movies, that guns had safety mechanisms, but apart from that he was clueless.

The dread he felt, and that had settled in his stomach, was now spreading. It seemed as though he had somehow swallowed a bucket of ice-cold water. What the hell had happened tonight? Somewhere after dinner with Craig and their drive to the old lookout point things had gone awfully wrong.

Hunter stopped the car. Jake looked outside and saw they were parked right in front of the only hotel in town, the very place he'd planned to crash just a few minutes ago. He didn't know what Hunter had planned, but maybe this was his opportunity. Maybe he could somehow make a run for it and ask for help.

Hunter turned off the engine and grabbed the gun. "Look at me," he said, tapping Jake's knee with it. Jake stiffened and turned his head to Hunter, who locked eyes with him before continuing: "This is how it's gonna be. We're going in there holding arms. You don't try to run, you don't ask for help. I would prefer not to hurt you. Don't make me pull this trigger." His voice was almost a whisper, which made it even more threatening.

"Why are you doing this?" Jake asked in a feeble voice he didn't recognize.

Hunter scoffed. "Why? What do you mean, why? Did I say you could leave me? Huh? You've embarrassed me, Jake. What'll our friends say?"

A chill ran down Jake's spine. He was starting to believe that Hunter was actually insane.

"Come on. Get out of the car," Hunter said, waving the gun at him.

Jake tried to unbuckle his seatbelt but his hands were shaking violently. His fingers couldn't press the release button hard enough.

"Move!" Hunter shouted.

Jake jumped. "I can't…this thing won't budge," he pleaded, fumbling around with the latch.

"Don't tempt my patience, Jake."

Jake took a deep breath, trying to calm himself down, and forced his fingers against the release button. It gave, and he was finally free.

They both got out of the car. Hunter approached him and held his arm like they were a happy couple, hiding the gun inside his coat. It had started to rain again, a drizzle, not quite enough to drench you immediately but annoying and cold. Jake's heart thumped inside him and his mind raced, still trying to spot an escape route. But there didn't seem to be one. Hunter's arm was intertwined with his own, holding him tight, and he could feel the gun's barrel against his ribcage. Maybe Britta would call the police after discovering he was not in his room. But it was hopeless. By then, who knows where they'd be?

As they walked to the hotel, the thought that this was all his own fault anyway and that he deserved it crossed his mind. It served him right for being weak and putting his happiness in the hands of others. *Shut up! Just shut up and stop with this stupid self-pity. If you're not happy, then stop doing what you've done your whole life!* Jake felt angry. The voice was right. He should stop belittling himself and start acting differently. The problem was he didn't know what to do to escape Hunter.

"Don't try anything," Hunter warned as they approached the hotel.

The automatic doors swooshed open and they entered the lobby. It reeked of cheap carpet shampoo and, for some reason, lemon. There was no one in sight, so Jake's hope of maybe asking for help withered on the spot.

Hunter dragged an increasingly pale Jake through the lobby. His hands were cold and wet and his heart raced like he'd just run ten miles. He felt dizzy and nauseated and was becoming progressively more desperate. When they walked by the concierge counter, Jake was still sweeping the room for any exits, as surreptitiously as possible. He was so focused on doing this that he almost didn't hear the concierge call his name.

"Jake? Hey, how are you?"

Hunter's arm squeezed Jake's and he almost froze in his tracks. Jake felt the pressure but only then noticed the greeting. He looked over his shoulder and saw Michael. He couldn't believe his luck. Maybe he could somehow make him see he was in trouble. He had to.

"Hey, Michael. How are things back at the clinic?" he asked in a raspy voice, open-eyed and somehow trying to will Michael to see he needed help. His voice had broken at the end of his reply and Hunter's arm tightened its grip. They were a couple of steps away from the counter and Hunter didn't seem eager to stay there, chit-chatting.

"The same, you know... I'm sorry, are you feeling well? You look sick," Michael said, furrowing his brow. "Can I get you something? A water maybe?"

Jake opened his mouth to speak but Hunter cut him short. "He's fine. I'm sorry but we have to go," he said, grinding his teeth.

Michael's gaze hopped from Jake to Hunter. He seemed unsure what to do for a second. "Sorry, sir. Have a nice evening."

Hunter yanked Jake's arm and almost dragged him away towards the elevators.

"Nice to see you again," Jake managed to call back over his shoulder, his eyes desperate, a lone tear falling down his cheek, "and give my best to Britta. Congratulations again on your baby, Michael."

He saw Michael's puzzled expression. It'd been a stupid thing to say, but Jake couldn't think of anything else. He just hoped Michael could recognize from this that he was in danger.

Hunter jerked his arm again and Jake turned his head away from Michael.

"What the hell was that back there?" Hunter whispered in a menacing tone when they stopped in front of the elevator.

"What do you mean?" Jake shuddered uncontrollably, like he had a bad fever. Had Hunter noticed his plea to Michael?

"How do you know that guy?"

"From high school… I ran into him the other day." Jake's feeble voice was breaking. His throat was dry and he found it hard to talk.

Hunter frowned, his gaze perusing him like he was trying to read his mind, find a lie in what he'd just told him, but he said nothing. The elevator dinged and the doors opened. Hunter pulled Jake inside and pressed the button for the third floor.

"You'd better not try anything."

CHAPTER 21

THEY ENTERED HUNTER'S room and Jake saw a duffel bag filled with clothes in the corner, and a couple of shirts and jeans spread out on the bed. It was obvious he hadn't spent much time in here since he'd arrived. Hunter pushed him further into the room and locked the door.

"Stay in that corner while I pack," he barked, pointing a finger at the opposite wall.

Jake dashed to the wall and leaned on it. He was still trying to find an escape, but there was none. To get to the door he'd have to run past Hunter and his gun, and the window was of no use. It was closed and they were on the third floor.

He leaned on the wall and willed himself to take long, deep breaths, trying to calm himself down. He watched as Hunter hurried through the room, grabbing his things and putting them into the duffel bag. Jake's heart rate was finally slowing and he concentrated on the cold of the wall. He imagined Hunter dying in a thousand different ways. That creep, that jerk, that awful, disgusting scumbag. He was mad at the injustice of the situation; the injustice of having someone presuming he was their property and had to do whatever they wanted. Jake imagined himself flying at Hunter's neck, punching him in the face repeatedly until he understood he wasn't a thing for him to carry around.

"Are you aware of what you're doing? Do you realize this is kidnapping?" he pleaded. The courage he'd had to summon just to utter those words made his heart rate race again and left him panting.

"Just shut up!" Hunter said, turning his menacing eyes on him before resuming what he'd been doing.

Jake felt anger bubbling up inside him. "If you let me go now it won't be too late, Hunter. Think about what you're doing. This is insane! Do you want to ruin your life?" His voice wasn't breaking as much anymore.

"Shut up, Jake! Just shut up!" Hunter shouted, approaching him. "Now you're worried about my life? Now? After leaving me like that? Without a word?" Hunter turned his back on him and scoffed, before looking back at him again. "Do you have any idea what I've been through? The humiliation? I went everywhere, Jake. Everywhere! I even tried to file a missing persons report at the police station but they just laughed at me. Laughed! I spent a sleepless week talking to everybody I could remember. Nobody knew anything. And then—then—I go to your buddy Matt's house and what do I find? That you left me! That you decided to go away without so much as a word. And now you're worried about me and my life?" Hunter had been steadily talking louder and louder, now yelling.

Jake felt Hunter's rage hit him like a brick wall. His own anger bubble burst and, in its place, that familiar dread appeared. Hunter turned his back on him again and paced the bedroom.

"You didn't give me any alternative," Jake said in a feeble tone. "Do you know how my life has been this past year? Your jealousy is completely insane. You never let me go anywhere without making a scene. You forbade me from seeing my own friends, of going out. You were always yelling at me and I was afraid you would beat me. You got really aggressive, you know that? What else could I do? I tried to talk to you but you wouldn't listen." Jake felt utterly idiotic for telling him all this.

It was the ultimate irony, to make Hunter see how aggressive and insane he was when he'd just kidnaped him.

Hunter turned to him again and tilted his head sideways. "You tried to talk to me? There's nothing to talk about," he said, slowly approaching Jake. "You said you loved me, remember? I took care of you, I bought you presents, I helped you when nobody cared about you. You're mine. You have to understand that." Hunter's eyes were squinting. "Do you know how lucky you are for having me? Do you? Not many can brag about being with an assistant professor. I'll be a headmaster someday. I can't have you running away from me and humiliating me like that. What will people say?" He shook his head and again turned his back on Jake, walking away. "You made me act like this. If I was jealous it's because you gave me a reason to be. And if I ever screamed at you, it was because I loved you and I cared about you. You made me do all of this. I wouldn't be angry if you hadn't left me," he said, looking over his shoulder.

Jake listened to him saying that it was all his own fault and felt something inside him snap. A geyser of hot-red lava sprung to life in his gut, spreading through him. "I'm making you do what? Be an asshole? What kind of a deranged argument is that?" He immediately regretted his remark, but it was too late. He'd said it without thinking, driven by the molten rock in his gut.

He cowered and pulled his arms up, trying to stop Hunter's slap but it was too late.

"Don't you dare speak to me like that! You hear me? I don't want to hit you but I promise I will if you continue talking like that."

Jake's bubbly anger fizzled and morphed into fear as he watched Hunter towering over him, a menacing stare in his eyes. For a second, he'd forgotten that Hunter was acting like a lunatic and was dangerous, maybe to the point of actually using the gun. Jake touched his face, trying to ease the burning pain of Hunter's powerful slap. A couple of tears got the best of him and escaped despite his efforts to hold them back. He felt helpless and at the mercy of someone he didn't recognize anymore. This was way beyond the jealous Hunter, the guy who had thrown a tantrum or yelled at him when he'd decided to have a coffee with friends. How could he have been so naïve and blind for so long? How could he have not seen Hunter for who he really was?

Hunter returned to his duffel bag and Jake sat on the armchair near the bed. He let a couple of tears slide down his cheek in silence and watched as Hunter packed his bag. He couldn't believe his fate would be this life of fear in the claws of someone so revolting. This couldn't be it; there still had to be something he could do to get help. He couldn't believe Hunter really was going to kidnap him and that there was nothing anyone could do about it.

Someone knocked three times on the door. Hunter stopped rummaging through his things and straightened instantly, like someone had whipped him on his back.

"Who is it?" he called out.

"Room service," someone said.

Hunter turned to Jake. "Stay there. Quietly," he whispered.

He took the gun, held it behind his back and approached the door, opening it. "I didn't order—"

Hunter didn't have the chance to finish his sentence. The door swung open violently, knocking him back and sending him flying. Hunter landed on the floor with a loud thud, grunting hard as the shock expelled the air from his lungs.

Craig entered the room the next second, open-eyed and panting, sweeping the place frantically. His eyes locked on Jake, a mixture of relief and pain on his face. "Jake!" he shouted, dashing over to him. "Are you okay?" Craig asked even before reaching him.

"He has a gun!" Jake said, pointing a trembling finger at Hunter. Craig stopped and looked back. Hunter's gun had flown from his hand and landed on the floor, almost sliding under the bed. Craig saw its barrel at the same time Hunter was getting up.

Their eyes met and they both dashed to the bed. Hunter's hand was almost on the gun, but Craig grabbed him by his waist and pulled him back and away from the bed. Hunter balanced himself and the two measured each other up for a second. They were both tall, Hunter the taller of the two. But Craig seemed stronger.

After a moment's indecision, Hunter threw himself forward, grunting. His fist flew towards Craig who managed to dodge it, its momentum carrying Hunter off balance. Craig seized the opportunity and jabbed his elbow into Hunter's back, sending him against the wall. Craig now grabbed Hunter by his shoulders, turned him around and punched him on the jaw. When Craig went in for a second punch, Hunter grabbed his hand and kicked him on his leg. Craig cringed and backed away, Hunter taking the opportunity to run from the room. Craig limped after him as fast as he could.

Now alone in the room, Jake wasn't really sure what had just happened. It had happened so quickly. Was it safe to leave? Nobody was there to answer him, the room and the hallway beyond both totally silent.

He got up from the chair and took a few, tentative steps. He tried to hear if it was safe to leave, but his drumming heartbeat got in the way.

Then he heard Craig returning at a run, soon back in the room. "I lost him. Did he hurt you?" he asked, grabbing Jake by his shoulders, his eyes scanning him frantically.

Jake couldn't answer. He wanted to speak, but couldn't. He shook his head as a sob escaped him.

Craig held him in his arms. "It's okay. I'm here," he said.

In that moment, Jake couldn't care less about the text message or what a big jerk Craig had been. Now he didn't even remember it. His mind was blank, engulfed in the relief of Craig being with him.

CHAPTER 22

SOMEWHERE, THERE WAS a bird making a noise. Singing. Loudly. Was it a blackbird? And although Jake's eyes were shut, the light was almost unbearable. Why was the light on? Had he forgotten to turn it off last night? Last night... He couldn't remember which day it was or what had happened the night before. He searched his mind for a second but came up with nothing. His memory was an opaque mystery he couldn't infiltrate.

Jake opened his eyes but squinted, overwhelmed by the bright light that now hurt his eyes even more. He blinked several times while his vision adjusted, before realizing the intense light was actually just a dim ray of sunlight, slipping through heavy curtains. He looked around. This was Britta's home, the room he'd been staying in. Jake searched for his phone. 1 p.m. *Fuck! I'm late to—*

In that moment his memory came rushing back and he remembered everything; Hunter pointing a gun at him, the fear of being taken somewhere nobody would ever be able to find him, Craig thundering through the door and saving him. The relief he'd felt when he'd seen him had been overwhelming. He hadn't been able to speak and practically fainted when Craig brought him home. Maybe it was a way of his body coping with all the stress, but he barely remembered falling into bed.

He wanted to rescue me after last night? Jake couldn't understand why Craig had gone after him if he knew he'd seen the text message. What was he trying to prove? *Stop, just stop.* He should stop nurturing these obsessive, self-loathing thoughts. It didn't do him any good. *If you want to know, just ask him.*

Jake got out of bed and stretched. He approached the window and opened the curtains. It had stopped raining and the sun was even trying to smile from behind the clouds.

After a quick brush of his teeth, Jake left the room and went downstairs. The house was silent but for muffled voices coming from the kitchen. He opened the door. Craig and Britta were sitting on stools, talking by the kitchen counter. Their heads both turned his way.

"You're up. How are you feeling, honey?" Britta said, her voice breaking. She seemed about to burst into tears. Craig watched him enter the kitchen in silence.

"I'm okay, I guess. Why didn't you wake me up? It's late."

Jake walked to the counter and sat opposite Craig.

"You seemed exhausted yesterday. You barely spoke when Craig brought you in and then you immediately fell asleep as soon as you hit the bed. We thought it would be best to let you rest, considering… Well, considering what you've been through."

Jake pulled his lips into a half-smile. Images from the previous night flashed in his mind, a downpour of feelings and emotions that threatened to overwhelm him. He pursed his lips as he remembered the gun pointing at him, the helpless feeling… Was it his fault? Was he the one to blame for Hunter's deranged actions?

"Do you want something to eat?" Britta touched Jake's shoulder and he shuddered. Her face contorted into a look of remorse. "Are you okay?"

"I'm fine. Don't worry." He took a deep breath. "Yes, I would like to eat, thank you. I'm hungry."

Britta smiled and hurried to the fridge. "I'm gonna prepare you some eggs."

Craig still watched Jake in silence, a delicate smile spreading across his face. "Jake," he finally said, looking down. "I know that maybe this is not the best time, but I'd like to talk about that message you saw yesterday." His eyes were now level with Jake's, his gaze perusing his soul.

Jake's stomach did a somersault. "You don't have to explain anything. It's your life, really…"

"I know I don't have to, but I want to. I don't want you to get the impression I was deceiving you. I didn't lie to you, Jake. I'm not seeing anyone. I'm really not. That message was from a guy I used to date. He's been obsessed with me ever since and sends me these really inappropriate messages. I've already warned him not to, but I think he can't help himself when he's feeling lonely or something."

The gloom oppressing Jake's back started to lift. "So…you're telling me I'm not the only one with a crazy ex?" Suddenly, the whole subject now seemed funny and he felt compelled to laugh. The fear inside him subsided and Hunter didn't seem so dangerous anymore. This whole ordeal was starting to look like a bad dream, a distant memory.

Craig chuckled. "I guess you could say that. But your ex is way crazier. Mine hasn't tried to point a gun at me." Jake's smile instantly disappeared. "I'm… I'm sorry. I didn't mean to… It was a bad joke, sorry."

"Almost funny, Craig. Almost. Maybe in a few weeks?" he said, his eyebrows lifting up into an almost cheerful expression.

"Speaking of crazy," Britta said, from by the stove, "we were waiting for you to wake up to decide what to do regarding Hunter. Do you want to go to the police? I think you should."

"I don't know… I mean, it's my word against his."

"No! You have witnesses. You're not alone in this."

Jake now realized he still didn't know how Craig had been able to find him.

"How did you know where I was?" he said, looking at Craig.

Craig opened his mouth to speak but Britta was faster. "It was the power of love!" she said, all giddy and giggling.

Craig frowned. His face was flushed. He looked again at Jake. "You have to thank the concierge at the hotel. What's his name, Britta?"

"Michael."

"Yeah, Michael. He called Britta last night when he saw you with Hunter. He said you were pale and seemed scared, not to mention the fact you were not making any sense. So, he called to see if she knew what was going on."

"I was desperately trying to tell him I needed help without Hunter realizing it," Jake said with half a smile.

"Well, it worked. As soon as Britta heard Hunter's description I drove as fast as I could. What we still don't know is how he got into the house. Britta's been a bundle of nerves since last night because of it."

Jake felt his heart sinking. "He didn't come in. It was my fault. I was…feeling…like I couldn't breathe. I had to get out. So I climbed through the window and jumped onto the shed roof."

"Oh, my gosh, Jake. You could've gotten hurt!" Britta said.

"I told you no one had broken in, Britta."

"I'm sorry. I didn't mean to upset you," Jake said, feeling guilty.

"Let's change the subject, okay? What's done is done. What's important is that nobody got hurt. But I still think you should go to the police, Jake. Hunter might try something again."

Jake sighed. "I don't want to talk about it right now."

"If you don't want to talk, you'll have to eat. Here." Britta put a plate of scrambled eggs in front of Jake. It smelled wonderful and he realized how hungry he was.

"This is delicious. Thank you," he said, between mouthfuls.

"I'm glad you like it."

"Umm, Jake? I have something else to say to you," Craig said, playing with his thumbs.

Jake's heart sank and he put his fork back on his plate. He didn't know what it was, but he knew Craig would say something to break his heart. *Stop it. I mean it. Don't jump into negative conclusions. The message didn't mean anything, remember?*

Britta's gazed hopped from Craig to Jake, before she said, "I'll let you boys alone," and left the kitchen.

"I really don't want to, but I have to return to San Francisco," Craig said when Britta had left. "But remember our talk at the lookout point? I mean it, Jake. I don't want to leave you behind."

Jake's heart thumped in his chest.

"I know it's all too much right now, with Hunter and what you went through, but I wanted..." Craig's gaze travelled from Jake to his own thumbs, then back to Jake. "I wanted you to consider coming with me—and before you say no, please think about it. I know it's probably too much to ask of you, but I think I love you," he said in one go, like he was afraid he'd lack the courage to say it if he didn't rush it all out in one go. "No, that came out wrong. I don't think, I know I love you. And I know it's crazy and that it's only been a week since we met again, but I love you. I can't explain it, I just do. When that guy from the hotel called, I felt sick to my stomach. I can't imagine myself away from you, Jake. And I don't know why. I just know I can't."

Jake had stayed silent the whole time Craig had spoken. He couldn't believe Craig felt that way. He knew from their brief time at the lookout point that Craig cared for him, but love? Craig loved him? For a moment, Jake felt like the happiest man alive. After all, Craig loved him! But his dread came racing back. He suddenly feared he wasn't good enough for him. Did he have anything to offer Craig?

"I... I don't know what to say."

"Say yes."

Jake watched him. Craig eyes pleaded in silence and Jake felt touched. There was a barrage of feelings inside him that he couldn't process, but they were all pressing him to cry. What was wrong with him?

"I... I should be beyond thrilled. Back in high school I dreamed of us being together. When I saw you here, after all these years, my heart almost stopped and I felt my crush for you appearing again out of nowhere. I realized I loved you when I didn't know what you felt about me." Craig's eyes lit up. "But, I'm scared. Why do you love me? I'm not a particularly interesting person. I bet you can get a guy a million times better than me in no time, and I'm afraid you'll see that's so if I go with you. I'm afraid you'll realize that I'm not the guy you think I am. I don't want to suffer, Craig. I don't think I could survive it."

Craig seemed hurt by his words. "You know, when you first told me you had come here because you had no money and no work prospects, the first thing that crossed my mind was 'why?'. Why was it that you chose to come here when you could have gone anywhere else? But then you told me about your mother and I understood. You're a good person, Jake, and that's rare to find. Why do you think I'm alone? Yeah, you're right. There are lots of guys out there who look like they came straight out of an Abercrombie catalog. But have you ever spoken to them? Do you know that most have nothing inside their heads? I don't want to be with a self-involved asshole, Jake. I want to invest in someone who has a heart. And you have one. Am I wrong?"

Jake's eyes welled. All these feelings he had inside him were now swirling in a hurricane of emotion. His old voices were telling him not to go with Craig, that he would be sorry when Craig found out he wasn't good enough.

Suddenly, Jake realized what he was doing. He was playing the victim, acting like he wasn't worth it, like he had done a million times before. It was his way of coping with pain. If you don't expect anything from life, you can't get hurt, right? He was so used to it he didn't notice it anymore.

He remembered the pact he'd made with Britta. They were going to be the captains of their own destiny. He had to ignore the voices. They could go fuck themselves.

"You know what? I am a good person. I've spent all my life trying to prove to the wrong people that I am someone who deserves to be happy, and all I did was end up thinking I didn't. But I do! I do deserve to be happy. And I love you, Craig. I love you so much it hurts."

Jake had a couple of tears running down his face by the time he'd finished talking, but they were tears of happiness. They were tears that symbolized that he was finally learning to let go of the shackles that had for so long dragged him down and made him believe he wasn't good enough.

Craig grinned and Jake let himself be bathed in his welcoming smile. Craig got up and drew near him. He looked deeply into Jake's eyes and kissed him tenderly, a soft kiss that sent ripples through Jake's body, cleansing him of all his grief.

Somewhere, in the distance, someone was banging at a door. It seemed urgent but Jake's mind dismissed it. He was completely lost in the bliss of that kiss.

Britta entered the kitchen a minute later and they stopped kissing. "I'm sorry. Jake?" she said, her voice quivering.

Jake thought she was trying hard not to cry, judging by her puffy eyes.

"Jake, honey, your father's in the living room…"

A bad feeling invaded Jake as adrenaline rushed through him, concentrating in his stomach. It felt like iced water. "What's happened? Why is he here?" he said, getting to his feet.

"It's your mother… I'm sorry," Britta said, tears running down her face.

Jake felt the ground disappear beneath him and rushed past Britta.

No!

CHAPTER 23

JAKE FLEW THROUGH the kitchen doorway, his heart thumping hard against his ribcage. He wanted to believe it was all a misunderstanding, that his father had failed properly to explain what he was doing here. The man was pacing the living room, grabbing his hair like he wanted to rip it out.

"Dad? What's happened?" he said, stopping inches away from him, trying to catch his breath.

His father stopped in his tracks and turned to face Jake. His eyes were red and almost popping out, his face contorted in anger. Jake had never seen him like this before, not even in his worst hours.

"You killed her! You killed her!" he shouted, advancing on Jake, his hands outstretched to him.

Jake took a couple of steps back, shaking his head in confusion. "What?" His voice was broken. He couldn't process his words. "Mom is... mom is..." Britta was right? His pain burst into a sob. His legs faltered and he fell to the floor.

"She was fine yesterday, before you took her to the clinic. And now... now... It's all your fault. Your fault!" he screamed. "God is punishing me for having an abomination like you for a son." Little balls of spittle had formed in the corners of his mouth as he spoke.

Britta and Craig came running from the kitchen.

"What's going on?" Craig asked in a thundering voice.

Jake was curled up on the floor, rocking back and forth while his father shouted that he was to blame for his mother's death. Craig ran to them and grabbed Jake's father by an arm, pulling him away from Jake.

"Please, sir, you have to calm down. You can't blame Jake for what's happened."

The man's gaze hopped from Jake to Craig. "Who are you to tell me what I can or can't do? I'm not going to be lectured by a brat."

"I just want you to calm down. Shouting won't help." Craig's face was tense, like he was avoiding saying something he would regret later.

"You're one of them, aren't you? One of those sodomites. Is that it?" the man asked, sneering at Craig.

Craig's face turned crimson red. "That's enough, sir. I think it's time for you to leave."

"I'll leave when I want to!"

Jake listened to the arguing, completely detached from the experience, as if he were tuning into a sad show on a strange TV channel. His father's words were still sinking in, but his brain couldn't quite process their meaning. He couldn't accept that his mother had died and he wouldn't be able to tell her how much he loved her; that despite him being miserable in his teen years, he didn't blame her. If anything, he was sorry for not being stronger and helping her live a different life, one far away from this man who wasn't sensitive enough to appreciate what he had and, instead, chose to live by his ignorance and fears.

"No, sir," Craig continued. "You'll leave now. This isn't your house and you're not welcome here if you only know how to offend and humiliate people."

The man scoffed. "I knew you were one of those sissies. Everything offends you! A man can't say his peace. But, then again, you're not really a man, are you?"

Something snapped inside Jake. He got up and walked past Craig. "That's enough! What's wrong with you?" he said in a voice so firm he hardly recognized himself. "Why do you keep doing this? Don't you see you're gonna end up all alone?"

"I've got God at my side," he answered in a firm tone, raising his chin.

"Stop with that nonsense. Do you realize what you're saying? Do you really believe God wants you to be this hateful?" Jake's nostrils now flared. He was angry but also saddened.

"I'm defending God's law on earth. Someone has to do something. This country is becoming overrun by sinners and sodomites."

"I pity you, I really do. You know why? Because now you'll be alone. You won't have mom there to put up with your shit and act like an emotional punch bag. Have you thought of that? I think you have. I bet that's why you're acting like this. Deep down you know you don't have any friends and everyone hates you. But you know what? It's all your own fault. You chose to be this awful person you are, don't forget that. You're always threatening me with the fires of hell, but you know what? Hell's right here on earth. Hell is what you put me through when I was a child, when I looked into your eyes and saw nothing but contempt. But I'm through with trying to earn your love and only managing to get stepped on in the process. I won't suffer anymore because you think I'm a sinner. Now, leave. These people don't deserve your bitterness. Go ask for forgiveness from your God. Maybe there's still time to get it."

Jake's father had listened, open mouthed. His face had gone from purple, to pale and back to purple again. "You'll burn in hell for this, you ungrateful fag—"

Craig grabbed Jake's father by his shoulder and hauled him to the front door. The man struggled but Craig was both taller and stronger. There wasn't much he could do beyond being dragged. Craig opened the door and pushed him out onto the porch, slamming the door behind him.

The moment had passed and so had Jake's newfound strength. The truth sank in, the meaning of it all, and he felt more alone now than he'd ever felt before. He slumped to the floor and cried. He cried for his mother who didn't deserve what had happened to her, and for not being able to ever see her again. But most of all he cried for himself and the sense of loneliness that had so cruelly invaded him, that now froze his gut and chest. He felt truly and utterly alone and was scared.

A warm hand touched his back and Jake was pulled from the void into which he was falling. He felt heat spreading through him, comforting him, and found himself again in this world. He looked up and saw Britta's worried gaze and Craig's gentle smile.

"It's okay," he said. "We're here for you."

Jake couldn't speak. He nodded and let Craig's love embrace him. The ice inside him began melting and Jake reminded himself that things were different, now. He had Britta. And he had Craig.

CHAPTER 24

A BIG ROLL of clouds clung to the mountains, embracing them and hiding their peaks. The trees on the street danced in the wind, touching each other with each strong gust. It hadn't yet started to rain but its promise was ever present.

Jake sat on the armchair close to the window, looking outside. A small patch of blue pierced the cotton-like sky and the sun shone through. He enjoyed the faint sunlight with his eyes closed and counted the minutes until he would be with Craig again.

A month had passed since his mother's funeral, thirty days in which Jake had fought hard to heal himself, to let the sorrow go. There was nothing he could do for his mother, only for himself. Britta had told him this countless times, but he wouldn't listen. In those first few days he could only hear the pain that told him he would never see her again. It had been an uphill battle fighting those thoughts. But then, one day, it had dawned on him: he'd spent his entire life fleeing from those who inflicted pain on him, trying to stay away from everything that was uncomfortable. And for what? In the end his mother had died anyway and he hadn't even been there for her. This renewed his resolve to follow the promise he and Britta had made to each other: they were the captains of their own destiny. Jake didn't want to sail anymore at the mercy of life's fickle winds. He wanted to take responsibility for what happened to him, to decide where to go next.

In that month, Jake tried to let go of all the anger he felt towards his father. It wouldn't do him any good. He'd even tried to talk to him and make amends, but his father wasn't quite ready for that yet. So, he just focused on what was important: Britta and Craig. Craig had been in San Francisco for a month, working like a madman so his boss would let him take a couple of days off earlier than scheduled. He'd had to return to his work and so hadn't been here for the funeral, but Jake hadn't minded. He knew where Craig's heart was. Plus, he was coming back for him and they'd soon be together in San Francisco, starting a new life.

Clouds covered the blue patch of sky again and Jake opened his eyes. He might as well finish packing. He got up from his chair at the same time as someone knocked on the door.

"Are you ready?" Britta asked, entering the room.

"Yup," he answered, smiling. They were going to the market to buy oranges. For some reason he was craving them and decided he had to buy a few for the trip.

"Guess who just called?" Britta asked as they left the room. "My jerk of a husband. And if I told you what he said to me, you wouldn't believe it." Britta scoffed as a half-smile crept onto her face.

Things between Britta and her husband had not improved over the past month. He'd been there briefly to pick up a few clothes but that had been it. Britta had been as civilized as possible but Jake could see how much she was suffering.

"He wants you to leave the house," Jake guessed as they went downstairs.

Britta snorted. "Even better. He says he's sorry and wants to try again. Can you believe that? After being for God knows how long with that bimbo, he wants to try again. She probably got fed up of him and gave him the finger. And I don't blame her."

They left the house and got into the car.

"What are you going to do?" Jake asked as Britta drove them away from the house.

"What we've planned all along. I'm taking over my life. I'm not going back to him or that life. I wouldn't be able to forgive myself. Besides, how can I trust him now? No. I want to continue my studies and move on with my life."

Jake smiled. He could sense the sorrow in Britta's voice but she was also more determined than ever. "If that's what you want, you have my total support."

Britta turned her head briefly towards him and Jake saw her eyes welling up. She looked back at the road and sniffed. "I'm gonna miss you so much… Which is stupid, really, because a month ago I didn't even have you in my life."

Jake stroked Britta's arm gently. "Don't cry or you'll make me cry. I promise this time I'm not gonna disappear. I'll try to visit often and in between we'll Skype, okay?"

Britta parked the car and killed the engine. "Pinky promise?"

Jake smiled. "Trust me. I'm not gonna make the same mistake twice. I intend to keep my friends close, even if that's only digital communications close."

Britta's eyes lit up and they got out of the car.

The farmer's market teemed with people and their chatter, and Jake breathed in the wonderful aromas that were everywhere. The stronger notes were citrus, but he could also detect cheeses and cold meats, as well as the sugary scents of different kinds of cakes, brownies and sweets. It was like being in nose heaven. And the joy of the place proved contagious. People seemed happy just to be here. Maybe it was the colors and the smells, but there was definitely a low hum that could be felt on the skin, charging the body with good vibes. Jake's lips curled up without him noticing. It was maybe the first time in a month he'd felt this good. He breathed deeply and embraced the happiness around him.

"What are you going to do over there? That city is so expensive," Britta said as they walked past several colorful countertops, full of tempting foods.

"I'm gonna find a job somewhere, maybe in a coffee shop. I want something that doesn't take too much mental space so I can write when I come home."

"I'm glad you're following your dreams, you know? I bet you in a year I'll be friends with a famous writer! I just ask that you please don't forget about me, okay?"

"Don't be silly. You'll be on the dedication page of every book I publish." Jake's eyes were drawn by a big pile of oranges. "Oh, wait. Those look nice."

Jake was talking with the vendor about the different kinds of citruses when he felt someone touch his shoulder. He looked back and his smile vanished instantly. His heart skipped a beat and the ground disappeared from beneath him.

"Hello, Jake."

Britta also looked back when she heard the voice. "What the hell are you doing here?" she demanded, grabbing Jake by his arm. "Come on, Jake. Let's find a cop."

A small group of people were now watching them, suspicion on their faces.

"Wait, please. I just want to talk."

"Talk? There's nothing to talk about, Hunter. You're a criminal. Stay away from us." Britta pulled Jake's arm as she tried to walk away, frantically looking around for a police officer.

"Wait, Britta," Jake said, pulling her back. "Please, sir. There's no need for that," he said to the vendor. "It's okay." The man was already part way through dialing 911 on his cellphone. Jake returned his gaze to Hunter. It all seemed like a bad dream. "What do you want?"

"I know about your mother… I'm sorry."

"How dare you?" Britta said. "How dare you come here and pretend to be worried about him? The nerve! You're lucky I don't have my gun with me. You'd be dancing to a different tune."

"Look, I made a mistake—"

"Mistake? Ha! Are you nuts? You didn't make a mistake; you kidnapped him! I'm calling the police—"

"Britta, don't. Please, it's all right," Jake said, stroking her arm.

"But the police are after him."

"No, they're not."

Britta opened and then closed her mouth. "What do you mean, 'they're not'?"

Jake sighed. "I never pressed charges."

"You what? Why not?"

He sighed again. "I wanted to let go of everything that's negative. I don't want it in my life anymore, you know? I thought I'd be better off that way. After my mom's death everything kind of lost its importance, even what he did," Jake said, nodding his head towards Hunter.

"Well, that's very generous of you but I think it's a mistake, Jake. He's a lunatic and should be behind bars," Britta said, crossing her arms as she stared at Hunter. "How did you know we were here, anyway?"

"I followed you here—"

"You see?" Britta said, turning her head to Jake while pointing at Hunter.

"Look, I'm not gonna try to excuse what I've done," Hunter said. "But I'd like you to know I'm leaving you alone. For good."

Jake furrowed his brows. "What changed?"

"Your mother died. It's not fair of me to ask you to come with me. I have to let you grieve, Jake. Maybe in a couple of months we could talk about you moving in with me."

Britta had watched Hunter, open mouthed, and then looked at Jake. "You see? Lunatic!" she cried, stretching her neck in Hunter's direction.

Hunter observed Britta, half his face slightly contorted in a grimace, like she disgusted him. "Goodbye, Jake. Talk to you soon." And with this, he left.

"What the hell was that about? You see what you did? You should've pressed charges, Jake. Now only God knows what he'll be up to. He's been following us all this time? The guy gives me the creeps. Why didn't he come forward sooner? What was he waiting for?"

Jake listened to Britta in silence. Why did Hunter lay low for so long without saying anything? *"Maybe in a couple of months we could talk about you moving in with me"*. Maybe Hunter thought Craig was out of the picture. Maybe Hunter didn't know he was going to San Francisco to be with Craig. Whatever his reasons, Jake thought Britta was right. He should've pressed charges.

CHAPTER 25

"HELLO, ANYBODY HOME?" Craig asked, knocking on the door and letting himself in.

Jake's heart jumped at Craig's voice. He leapt up from the couch where he and Britta had been talking and raced over to him. He'd been waiting the whole morning for this. No, the whole month. His chest brimmed with excitement and happiness, overwhelmed by a joy he couldn't remember ever having felt before.

Craig grinned and put his duffel bag on the floor before Jake ran into his outstretched arms. They hugged in a warm, tight embrace that seemed to last forever. Jake wanted to absorb his essence, make up for all the time they had been away from each other. He let himself sink into those big arms that could carry him forever and buried his nose in Craig's neck, letting his manly aroma invade him. Jake was overwhelmed by a sense of relief and safety. All the troubles of the world were rapidly fading away.

"I missed you," Craig whispered in Jake's ear.

Jake's skin rose in goose bumps as he felt Craig's warm breath on his neck. A low electric hum ran through his skin, concentrating itself on the top of his head and down in his crotch.

"I missed you too."

Craig's lips brushed Jake's softly, a caress that more than made up for their time apart. Their kiss then moved the earth and shattered Jake's worries about bumping into Hunter that morning in the market. Craig tasted so sweet. Jake felt alive again. He pressed his body against Craig's, feeling his sturdiness. It was impossible to move him. He was as solid as a tree.

A faint sob interrupted the moment. Jake looked behind and saw Britta crying, a smile on her face.

"I miss you already," she said, mopping her tears with a paper tissue.

Jake's heart ripped in two. She seemed so lonely and frail. Jake felt like the most self-centered guy in the world for leaving her here. It was completely absurd to think it, though. A month ago he hadn't even been a part of her life and she'd managed to survive. A little voice told him that learning to let go of the good things was hard. But now Britta had him and his friendship.

He approached her and sat on the couch, hugging her. "Don't cry. I don't think I can leave you here as it is."

"I'm just happy for you guys. And it's not like you're moving to the other side of the world. I'll come visit. And you can ring me when you're in town."

"You better have your phone with you all the time because I plan to come visit my father often," Craig said, sitting himself next to her.

"You kids are my two favorite people in the world, you know that?" and she blew her nose. "Enough with the crying. It's supposed to be a happy day," she said, crying and laughing all the same. "You have a long trip ahead of you and I have a job interview today."

They all got up from the couch and huddled in a big group hug.

"You ready?" Craig asked.

"Let me just get my things."

Jake went into the bedroom that had been his home for the past month and thought of Einstein. Time really was relative. He felt like he'd lived in this room his whole lifetime. He grabbed his duffel bag and his wallet, and gave the place one last good look. It was completely silent, apart from faint street noises seeping in through the window. He felt comfortable and safe and wondered about this next chapter in his life with Craig. The nostalgia that had invaded him now vanished. He was going to be happy. After all, he had waited his whole life for this.

The End

Thank you!

Thank you for reading *Becoming Jake*. I hope you enjoyed it.

Please consider leaving a review on Amazon, as they help readers find new authors and books. All reviews are appreciated, either positive or negative. Thank you in advance for your time and effort!

Other books by James Lee Hard

Stripped Expectations

http://www.amazon.com/dp/B00UIQVH76

Blurb:

Hunky Mark is unemployed, penniless and living off the help of his friends. His life orbits around sex encounters that leave him with a bitter aftertaste. He went from skinny tall guy to hunk in a few years, after promising himself not to let anyone beat him again. But Mark still struggles with his self-image because underneath all of his muscles he still feels like a clumsy teenager.

His life starts to change when a stranger approaches Mark offering him a job as a stripper. Mark immediately dismisses it as another lame attempt at getting him laid. But his desperate need for money makes him think twice. He ends up surrounded by gorgeous men, his first true love and a past that just refuses to go away.

WARNING: This book contains explicit scenes of consensual sex between men as well as some graphic language. It is intended for a mature, adult audience.

The Groom, the Bride and the Best Man (short story)

http://www.amazon.com/dp/B00XRPBUF4

Blurb:

Scott loved Russell since the day they met in college. He was the perfect guy: manly, gorgeous and charming. He only had one problem: a long time girlfriend. But that didn't stop Scott from catching mixed signals from Russell since day one. Could those just be wishful thinking?

Things reach a cathartic moment during Russell's wedding rehearsal. In an episode of foolishness, Scott drinks too much and drops the bomb. It was his last chance to know if his gaydar was right all along.

Inspired on a true story, this 5.000 word short is fuelled with heated discussions and physical encounters that will engage readers into a small but enthralling plot.

WARNING: This book contains explicit scenes of consensual sex between men as well as some graphic language. It is intended for a mature, adult audience.

About the author

James spends most of his time looking at his computer screen, trying to summon the magical words that make the ingredients for a great story. He dreams about being able to move people and becoming a great writer one day.

He writes contemporary gay romance and erotica but he wants to write about much more. His mind is filled with sci-fi gadgets, swords, wizards and dragons and he has trouble trying to choose one theme. Maybe one day we'll read something starring sinewy heroes battling giant dragons in tight pants. But the romance will always be there. And the abs. And the happy endings – Jame's a sucker for them.

James draws inspiration from everyday life, books, movies, songs, pictures and much more. Almost everything can ignite his desire to write but not all will end up on his stories.

He is an indie author who relies on friends and a growing base of lovely beta readers to help him with his stories, ensuring that each book is better than the previous one.

Find him on Twitter under @jamesleehard or drop him a line at jamesleehard@gmail.com. You can also visit his site at www.jamesleehard.com and keep up with all the news.

Printed in Great Britain
by Amazon.co.uk, Ltd.,
Marston Gate.